PROSPEROUS
HIP HOP PRODUCER

THE
PROSPEROUS
HIP HOP PRODUCER

MY BEAT-MAKING JOURNEY FROM MY GRANDMA'S PATIO TO A SIX-FIGURE BUSINESS

CURTISS KING

MAURICE BASSETT

The Prosperous Hip Hop Producer: My Beat-Making Journey from My Grandma's Patio to a Six-Figure Business

The Prosperous Series #2

Maurice Bassett
P.O. Box 839
Anna Maria, FL 34216

Contact the publisher:
MauriceBassett@gmail.com

www.MauriceBassett.com

Contact the author:
www.CurtissKingBeats.com

Edited by Chris Nelson
Cover design by Carrie Brito

ISBN: 978-1-60025-119-1

Library of Congress Control Number: 2017964023

First Edition

A Note on QR Codes

Throughout this book you'll find QR codes you can scan to view or listen to additional content. QR code readers are usually available for free or at minimal cost from app stores. We've also provided links you can type directly into your browser to access the same material.

ACKNOWLEDGMENTS

To my mother, Rochelle, for believing in my dreams
and showing me the value of a giving heart.

M

To my dad, Keith, from whom I learned my tenacious work ethic.
Because of you I've known the difference between a leader
and a follower since I was a child. To my stepmom, Nicol.

M

To Grandma and Grandpa Howard and Burton.

M

To the love of my life, Domunique, and my son, Nahzier,
for being the supportive fuel that drives me daily.

M

To my siblings, Jazmine, Paige, Micaela, Kamau, & Imani.

M

To Keyden, for rapping over my beats when they were trash
and for being the big brother I never had.

M

To John, Victor, Tae Beast, Captain, Oh Gosh Leotus, Nabeyin, Big
Face Villain, Ghrimm, Jynxx, Willie B, & THX, for teaching me the
sacred art of producing. To OSYM Beats, for selflessly showing me
the business of leasing my beats which ultimately changed my life.

M

To Joshua, Sallis, Komboa, Art Barz, Dirty Birdy & Professor
Morgan, for being the greatest mentors I've had. To Murs, Prof,
Ab-Soul, TDE, Noa James, Lesa J, Dibia$e, Ace Pun, Glasses
Malone, & Street Goddess, for giving me a chance to be heard.

M

To Maurice, Ilona, and Chris, for giving me
the opportunity to share my story.

M

Curtiss King

TABLE
OF **CONTENTS**

PREFACE:
THE **PROSPEROUS**
HIP HOP PRODUCER

In life you will encounter many different types of people. Most will talk a good game. Others will critique the rules of the game and the players playing it. But people like me just clock in when their number is called and play the game to the best of their ability. We don't do much talking—we just keep our eyes on the prize and rarely concern ourselves with the affairs of others.

My name is Curtiss King. I am a rapper and producer from Southern California. I have been blessed to do what I do for over fifteen years now. I've had the opportunity to produce for artists such as Kendrick Lamar, Ab-Soul, E-40, and Murs. My production has been used by corporate giants like MTV, VH1, and VANS. Even so, you may or may not have heard of me, and that's perfectly fine. I'm glad you found your way to my book.

I'd like to say that I'm more than just my credits. I am a

hardworking, family-oriented man and friend. I'm the elder brother to three sisters and one brother. I'm a recovering workaholic. I'm a passionate creator of and listener to music from the soul. I am a go-giver. I am a luminary—or in other words, "one who inspires and fills others with light." I am a Hip Hop artist and producer coach. I am big brother Curtiss to many people around the world, thanks to YouTube. Above all, I am a man of value.

In this book I document the journey of how I went from making $80 a month creating beats from places like my grandma's patio or a friend's couch to six figures a year from the comfort of my own home. In my story, I hold no punches and I tell no lies. In some chapters I discuss never-before-told stories of my darkest and brightest moments as an aspiring producer. I take you from my early days as a seventeen-year-old making beats on my grandma's patio, to my first major-label placements, all the way up to my present day work as a Prosperous Producer.

In all honesty, I never saw myself writing a book about my journey at the young age of thirty-two. I always figured writing a book would be reserved for much later in my life. But I want to share stories I genuinely feel can provide value and motivation to aspiring producers. So *The Prosperous Hip Hop Producer* is a book designed to be both informative and autobiographical at the same time. I want my fellow producers to see the realities of pursuing a career in music production. Along the way I offer ideas about production, how to find work, how to get along with people in the business, and other tips that can help you in your own career.

What I *really* hope is that you discover lessons in my life story that you can use to get to where *you* want to be in yours.

The world is full of eager listeners and potential clients patiently awaiting your arrival. What better time to start than now?

What's a "Hip Hop Producer" anyway?

One thing before we officially dig in. Since the word "producer" means different things in different contexts, here are a few quick details about exactly what a Hip Hop Producer is—and does.

For starters, there's an enormous difference between a "beat maker" and an actual music producer. A beat maker's only job is to create beats, loops, melodic/percussive ideas, and starting points for artists and songwriters to write their songs to. Most times, beat makers are not involved in the actual recording process or arrangement of the final song. Music producers are much more hands-on. They can generally contribute significantly to every step of the process of song creation, including recording, directing live musicians, engineering the music, and presenting ideas that can make the final product as great as possible.

I have tremendous respect for both sides, and I myself have played both roles in my career.

CHAPTER 1

THE **TEMPO**

"I don't want no drummer. I set the tempo."

~ *Bessie Smith*

I was taught that every beat has a humble beginning. Every musical masterpiece begins with a simple idea. I became obsessed with this idea early on, and it kept me from quitting. Knowing this always brought me comfort as an aspiring producer. I think it's because I'm a chronic overthinker. I have a tendency to make things more difficult than they need to be. So when I first began dissecting the elaborate compositions of producers like Dr. Dre, J. Dilla, 9th Wonder, Timbaland, The Neptunes, and Organized Noize, I desperately needed to understand that any beat, no matter how complex and intimidating the final product sounds, has to start with something as simple as its *tempo*.

IN THE BEGINNING

I wasn't supposed to become a music producer. FLAT OUT! As a matter of fact, if it weren't for my best friend Keyden making that decision *for* me, I would probably have a much different story to tell. Where would I have been? My gut instinct tells me I'd still be pursuing a career in music as a rapper. But who knows?

Growing up I was more passionate about video games and doodling pictures of my favorite X-Men comic book characters. For all I know, Curtiss King could've easily been one of those guys on YouTube doing weekly reviews of vintage video games. You know the type I'm talking about! Guys with colorful, ridiculously-animated thumbnail previews, holding two thumbs up and wearing grins and bewildered stares only a mother could love. YES! That could've been me, but thankfully God had other plans for my life.

If you look up the word "prosperous" in the *Merriam-Webster* dictionary, it's defined as "having or showing success or financial good fortune." Now if you'd have told me when I began this journey at sixteen that by the age of thirty-one I'd be making a comfortable living selling my beats, I wouldn't have called you crazy. If you'd have told me that my beat-selling business would gross six figures in the first two years, I *still* wouldn't have called you crazy. I'd just have had two simple questions for you:

Did I become massively famous?

. . . and . . .

Why did it take me SO damn long?

You see, even at the age of sixteen I knew that I'd be successful in some capacity, no matter what career I chose to pursue. I always had a hunch that someday I would be a massively influential human being. The only question I had was "When will it finally happen?"

In 2001 I was an inquisitive sixteen-year-old kid. To many of my

Downey High School classmates I was seen as wise beyond my age. Many of my friends joked that I was an old man trapped in a young man's body. I think it had to do with the deep grandpa-ish tone of my natural speaking voice and the fact that I couldn't care less about the latest trends in fashion (mostly because I couldn't afford them). Most of my youth was spent more around my highly influential parents and grandparents than around kids my age.

However, to some of my other classmates I was the goofiest person they'd ever met. I've always LOVED to make people laugh. One of my biggest role models was Will Smith when he played in the popular 1990s TV show *Fresh Prince of Bel-Air*. This ability to make my high-school classmates laugh was always a major personal win for me because I grew up extremely shy.

So between these two personas, you can imagine I stood out in a major way. But I got used to being viewed as *different* and grew to embrace it. At first I didn't realize that being different was actually to my advantage, but I did know that my peers and I weren't into the same stuff.

While most of my classmates were excitedly discussing the Sadie Hawkins dance or where they hoped to go to college, I was doodling lyrics in my notebook. But I never viewed myself as a loner back then; I knew that at any given moment I could easily jump into any conversation, no matter the topic, and give my two cents. It also wasn't that I didn't like people, because I loved being around my classmates even if we did have different interests. In fact, I was that guy who knew at least one kid in every lunchroom clique. From the skaters, the revolutionaries, the athletes, the ROP kids, the goth kids, and even the hacky sack kids, I was known for showing love to anyone who showed me love back.

Most importantly, there was no way I could truly feel like a loner with a best friend like Keyden Thomas. Keyden was like a big brother to me. He too was an overthinker. Man, you want to talk about two teenagers with too much of the world on their brains? That was us. In 2001 we would take the Downey Link bus home and seamlessly wind in and out of conversations about the impending war in Iraq, Maxim models we would *wife up,* Ludacris's *Word of Mouf* album, and the Laker's chances of repeating as NBA champions.

We weren't your average high schoolers, at least not as far as we could see. We embraced our differences, but not for the sake of saying we were different. We simply moved at a different tempo than our peers.

This was even more evident to us when music took over our lives. And no, that's not an exaggeration. Music came in like a thief in the night and literally stole our young lives in 2001—all because of a dare.

THE BET THAT STARTED IT ALL

Yes, we started making music on a *dare.* One fateful night Keyden asked if I'd ever thought about rapping, and then dared me to write a rap verse in less than thirty minutes.

Rapping? I mean, I had written poetry for years, but the idea of rapping never really crossed my mind until that night. Confused, and even a bit nervous at the proposition, I said, "Why are you asking?"

"Never mind why I'm asking," Keyden replied. "It's 7:30 right now. I'm going to call you back at 8:00, so have a verse ready."

Ladies and gentlemen, that phone call exchange was the start of my rap career. I didn't even have an instrumental to write my verse to! It was just me and a blank, intimidating sheet of college-ruled paper. Somehow, someway, one word after another, I began churning out rap lines about absolutely nothing.

As promised, Keyden called me back at 8:00 p.m. sharp. He was so excited that he decided to rap first. I don't think I even wrote a full sixteen-bar verse, but as I waited for Keyden to finish reciting what he had written, I mentally prepared to share my own material. When my turn came, I nervously recited some scatterbrained rhymes that randomly referenced everything from Red Bull energy drinks to children's cartoons like *Blue's Clues.*

It was terrible, but it was a start. Keyden seemed to be a lot more excited about this journey than I was. Writing that verse took me out of my comfort zone and I found that extremely, well, *uncomfortable.* My voice was awkward, and my content was corny and all over the place.

But the more writing sessions he and I had over the next few months, the better we both became. Eventually we decided to form a rap group called Soulja Camp. Our mission statement was: **No matter where music takes us, we keep our family first. DO IT FOR THE FAM!**

Most of our early writing sessions were at Keyden's apartment, where he lived with his grandmother, dad, and younger sisters. I lived one floor up in the same apartment complex with my dad. I spent a lot of time at Keyden's place writing lyrics, watching music videos on BET, and playing video games. Perhaps this is where we were most like our peers at that age.

In fact, video games were a major part of our lives. Our favorite was a basketball game called *NBA Live.* Sometimes we'd play it as a team and other times in the most intense, potentially-friendship-ending, smack-talking, YOU-DON'T-WANT-NONE-OF-THIS, head-to-head battles against one another.

Most of our writing sessions were on the weekends when we didn't have the responsibility of homework breathing down our necks. We'd write to any beats I could find on the Internet—usually they were a simple Napster search away. Neither of us had a job, so we couldn't afford to buy original beats.

There were a few talented beat makers who went to school with us. Sometimes they'd reach out after seeing us practice freestyling while waiting for the bus.

For those unfamiliar with the art of freestyling, picture a group of aspiring rappers rapping the first rhyming lyrics they can think of without stumbling. This is better known as a "rap cypher." Sometimes our group included a producer who volunteered to beat box (create a beat using his or her mouth to keep the group cypher going). Keyden and I were really good at this, because whenever we couldn't record we would practice freestyling. Our ability to freestyle caught the attention of these producers, and they'd often exchange contacts with Keyden and me in hopes of collaborating. But when we followed up with them it was generally the same story: they were looking for a payday and saw us as nothing more than another dollar sign.

> *We knew that no matter how great our lyrics, voices, or song concepts were, nobody was going to listen to us if our beats were subpar.*

I remember some of these producers asking us for $300 to simply LEASE one of their beats. I'll explain later in this book about the ins and outs of leasing beats, but just know that to us this was the equivalent of paying a $300 car note for a car that anybody else could drive at any time.

I found a few original beats on a music-sharing website called MP3.com, but I soon noticed that most of them were cheesy attempts by up-and-coming beat makers to copy the more popular music of the time. Keyden and I knew early on how important the music we chose to rap over would be to our success. We also knew that no matter how great our lyrics, voices, or song concepts were, nobody was going to listen to us if our beats were subpar. So we agreed that until we could afford to purchase original production, we would rap on popular beats that all our friends would easily recognize.

In the early 2000s that meant 50 Cent instrumentals, Wu-Tang instrumentals, Black Star instrumentals . . . and pretty much any other instrumental of whatever song was popular at the time. Our decision was inspired by the then up-and-coming rapper 50 Cent and his group G-Unit, who were making a killing in the independent rap spectrum by rapping over the most popular instrumentals. At the time, G-Unit was virally spreading their unofficial remixes on compilation CDs called mixtapes. Keyden and I saw the potential for getting our name out there by doing the exact same thing, so we followed their lead. By using a popular file-sharing service called Napster, we were able to (illegally) download pretty much any instrumental we wanted.

Mixtapes vs. Albums

In case you're confused about the difference between a mixtape and an album, let me explain. Albums are generally meticulously arranged collections of music with very deliberate song placements. A mixtape, on the other hand, is traditionally a more loose approach to creating a project. Mixtapes are generally just as their name suggests: random mixtures of songs and styles based loosely around a theme or mixtape title.

Keyden figured out a way to record our voices over these beats using his dad's old cassette boom box. It was a fun but often tedious process requiring two cassette tapes and constant rewinding and listening to record each verse and adlib. In the beginning it took us some time to get used to the recording process, but we were super motivated by the prospect of becoming rappers.

Soon we became addicted to recording ourselves. Our regimen was as follows: Write a song over a popular beat, immediately record it, go eat some fast food, play four quarters of *NBA Live*, and start writing to a new beat. We did this religiously for about six months, until eventually we got burned out.

WE WANT OUR OWN BEATS!

Don't get me wrong: we LOVED the fact that we could record our thoughts and that we saw ourselves getting better and better, but we were getting tired of rapping over everyone else's beats. Not to mention, during that era every other up-and-coming rapper in our area was also following the 50 Cent and G-Unit mixtape formula.

Keyden and I would listen to local mixtapes other rappers passed to us in the mall and literally hear the same exact beats we were rapping over. My secret Napster website wasn't as secret as I'd thought it was.

For two kids who prided themselves on being different from their peers, this was a HUGE problem. We desperately needed original beats to separate ourselves from the herd of aspiring rappers. But what could we do? Neither of us had the money for original beats. At the same time we were sick and tired of rapping over other rapper's beats. We also didn't have the money for equipment to create original music.

Maybe many of you reading this think the most logical solution was to get jobs. I wish it had been that easy. Believe me, our parents aggressively encouraged us to get jobs and we genuinely wanted to earn our own money. But after submitting literally hundreds of applications and receiving hardly any callbacks, it was clear that jobs weren't immediate options in our city. Keyden and I talked all the time about what to do. I even asked myself if this dilemma would bring an end to our dream.

It's my belief that the moment I began asking myself questions like that out loud, God began to provide answers in the oddest places. A few days after Keyden and I had a long discussion, we were presented with an opportunity that literally changed our circumstances overnight. Ironically, this opportunity came to us in a video game store.

Lessons to Take Away from Chapter 1

1. Your success in this industry will ultimately be determined by the tempo you set from the beginning.
2. Embrace your differences and use them to your advantage.
3. Establish a strong work ethic early on in your career.
4. If you can, find an accountability partner to help you grow at your craft.

CHAPTER 2

THE SNARE

"The character of your beat is in your snare."

~ *J.Bizness*

In every single beat I produce, the snare always represents the foundation for the attitude I want to create within that beat. If I want the attitude of my beat to be authoritative and bold I'll use a heavy snare in a lower tone. If I want my snare to provide a fun and energetic landscape I'll use a clap or a snap. Every aspect of your snare, from its timing to the amount of reverb you put on it, communicates a different message to your listener.

NBA 2K3 OR MTV MUSIC GENERATOR?

Say what you will about video games being a waste of time. Remind me how every day they rot young brains around the world.

Tell me all the detrimental side effects they can have.

But it won't change the fact that a video game literally changed my life. No exaggeration.

It started with a random visit to a store called Electronics Boutique in the Downey Stonewood Mall. In October 2002, Keyden and I were excited about two things: making music and buying a new Sega Dreamcast basketball game called *NBA 2K3*. Keyden had upgraded his video game system to a Sega Dreamcast the prior Christmas, while I was still stuck with my outdated PlayStation 1. He and I collectively saved up our lunch money, birthday money, and Christmas money with the intention of going half on the new *NBA 2K3*. This arrangement of buying games for each other's consoles wasn't new to us because we spent most of our time playing one another.

The Stonewood Mall was so close to our high school that we could see the large "Stonewood" sign from our cafeteria. One day, after months of saving up the money we needed, we made "plans" to go to the mall after school to finally pick up *NBA 2K3*. Now, I put "plans" in quotes because when we arrived at Electronics Boutique we had no idea how those plans would really play out.

At first, that afternoon was no different from any other visit to the video game store. We demoed the games they had available in their glass box enclosures until we got bored and started looking elsewhere for new releases and gaming magazines. While Keyden made sure that the store still had copies of *NBA 2K3* available, I took a detour to the used PlayStation game rack. I'd discovered that the used game rack often presented inexpensive gems for dirt cheap. That day was no exception.

In the middle of this cluster of used PlayStation games I found a huge, blue, double-disc jewel case with an "MTV" logo on it. When I picked it up I didn't think much of it until I read its full title:

MTV MUSIC GENERATOR
Music Creation for the PlayStation

I thought to myself, *Who in their right mind would make music on a PlayStation?* The idea might have even made me chuckle a bit, but for some reason I was at least intrigued enough to continue reading. I nonchalantly flipped the game over and stopped on a sentence that made my heart jump into my throat:

Combine instrument sounds and riffs to create your own rock, Hip Hop, drum & bass, techno, house tracks and more.

"OH SH*T!"

Keyden overheard my reaction and asked me what was wrong. He already had *NBA 2K3* in his hand and was ready to go. I passed him the game and said, "This is exactly what we've been looking for."

Keyden looked it over and his eyes lit up like mine had. This game presented us with an opportunity. It was the answer to our current production dilemma. Here we were, two gamers and aspiring rappers with a very limited budget, staring at a game that promised to merge both our worlds.

Keyden's eyes panned back and forth indecisively between the two games. When he looked up at me the reality had settled in: we would have to make a big-boy decision. Even though *MTV Music Generator* was dirt cheap, we still couldn't afford to buy both games. I think most kids our age would have chosen the basketball game

> *Even then we knew that our decision had the power to affect our future in music.*

without any hesitation. However, as I stated earlier, Keyden and I saw ourselves as different. I think that maybe even then we knew on some level that our decision very likely had the power to affect our future in music.

We mulled it over, probably looking like contestants on *Jeopardy* when Alex Trebek cues the "Final Jeopardy" theme song. Keyden was the older and much wiser one in our duo, so I knew I was likely to lean towards whatever decision he made.

After careful thought he suggested we sleep on our final decision. We agreed not to buy either game until we talked it through.

So we returned the games to their respective racks and headed off to the bus station. On the way home we weighed the pros and cons of getting each game. We talked about where we currently were in our music careers and what it would take for us to get to the next level. We were undoubtedly passionate about advancing in music—but at the same time we were equally excited about the upgraded graphics and gameplay of our favorite video game series, *NBA 2K*. After all, we had saved our money for months in anticipation of getting *NBA 2K3*, but this other game was too important to ignore.

The more we talked about our situation that night, the more we realized just how serious we had become about our music careers. The pros of taking a chance on a game like *MTV Music Generator* far outweighed the pros of purchasing *NBA 2K3*. We knew, too, that *NBA 2K3* wasn't going anywhere anytime soon. Additionally, the love for creating music we'd started to develop was becoming more and more special to us. We knew that if we stayed on top of things we had the potential not only to change our own lives, but also the lives of our families. We kept reminding each other about the Soulja Camp mission statement: **DO IT FOR THE FAM.**

We decided to move on our decision. That next day at school was an absolute blur for me. I had tunnel vision. I didn't care about anything except eating and buying *MTV Music Generator* with Keyden after school. The girl of my high-school dreams could've professed her everlasting love for me and she would've looked like a possum compared to *MTV Music Generator*.

The moment I saw Keyden after school we started speed-walking towards the mall like senior citizens getting in their morning workout. We were HYPED, to say the least! All we talked about was what type of beats we wanted to make. It didn't matter that neither one of us had ever even attempted to make a beat before. When you're seventeen and THAT excited about something, common sense has a way of just flying out the window.

When we arrived at Electronics Boutique we headed straight for the discount rack. We searched and searched and searched for *MTV Music Generator*, but we couldn't find it. Unfazed, I decided to look around the store in case someone had moved it to another rack. Meanwhile, Keyden asked the cashier if the game was still available. With a diabolical smirk, the cashier pointed at the new release rack. And what do you know? Some asshole had decided not only to put *MTV Music Generator* on the new release shelf—but also to place it right next to *NBA 2K3*.

I looked at Keyden with a face that said, "You gotta be kidding me."

Maybe it was a coincidence, maybe it was a test, or maybe it was an evil Electronics Boutique employee who had placed these games next to one another after overhearing us struggle with our decision the day before.

Now our big-boy dilemma was even harder. When we'd been weighing the pros and cons of each game, one of the pros was the fact that if we went with *MTV Music Generator* we would walk away with more money in our pockets because it was significantly cheaper. Now the prices of the two games were identical.

Looking back now, I realize how defining a moment that was for my character. It was the first time I made a commitment to myself that no matter how inconvenient new circumstances appeared to be, I would always be prepared to readjust and make a wise decision.

We chose to go with *MTV Music Generator*.

It's my belief that when we made our choice something clicked inside our brains. Neither of us was in a rush to grow up, but we both had a passionate desire to take care of our loved ones. For us, music presented an opportunity to do that while also doing something we absolutely loved. Somewhere in the back of our adolescent brains we knew that this decision was bigger than the disappointment of missing out on *NBA 2K3*. We knew that playing that game wasn't going to put Keyden's grandmother in a mansion or my mom on an island where she could relax and never have to work another day in her life.

> **I made the commitment to myself that no matter how inconvenient new circumstances appeared to be, I would always be prepared to readjust and make a wise decision.**

You might think I'm sounding overdramatic regarding the struggles of two kids deciding between video games. But to the producers out there who truly know what's up, you'll understand the potential impact of this decision on our lives. This purchase was the equivalent of law school for the potential lawyer or police academy for the officer-in-training. *This game was the most important purchase I've ever made in my music production career.*

PARENTS JUST DON'T UNDERSTAND

The first week we had *MTV Music Generator* it went back and forth between our houses. Even though I didn't know exactly what I was doing with it, I was having fun learning the process.

Keyden? Not so much. I think he enjoyed the idea of creating original music, but not the tedious process that beat-making required.

Making beats isn't for everyone, especially the impatient. It requires a lot of energy and obsessive attention to detail. This is one of the main reasons many aspiring producers never reach their true potential. Most quit when their frustration becomes consistently greater than their excitement. I, on the other hand, was as excited as could be about the process.

I was addicted from the first time I loaded *MTV Music Generator* into my PlayStation 1. Every school night I rushed through my homework assignments just so I could get in a few extra hours of practice on it before bed. My parents had been divorced since I was a baby, so I was used to spending school semesters at my dad's apartment and school vacations at my mom's. At the time my dad was a middle school teacher who was extremely strict about education being my first priority. He wasn't excited about my passion for this new "game." To him, it served as a massive distraction from my ability to be a successful high-school student.

In all fairness, he wasn't wrong about that.

I completely understand—now—where he was coming from. Education was my dad's passion. He was pursuing a doctorate in education even as he taught. He worked hard and carried the weight of the world on his shoulders. Many times that stress had negative effects on our relationship. He set high standards for himself and expected others, including his son, to live up to the same. Like I say, I know now that it was because he loved me, but I didn't understand that at the time.

He wasn't *always* strict. We'd often spend time watching sports and working out together. And although he wasn't excited about my musical pursuits, we had one thing in common: an enormous appetite for success.

But the deeper I got into music, the more I started to realize that he and I had two completely different visions of what success looked like.

Ever since I was a kid, almost everything I did was to make my dad proud. From competing in Little League Baseball, to learning Tae Kwon Do, to eventually starting to make music, I wanted to impress him and live up to his standards. So it was difficult explaining to him that the reason I wasn't currently job hunting was so I could make music on my PlayStation. Imagine trying to explain to your dad in the early 2000s, before social media, how spending hours and hours on a video game could one day help you make a comfortable living.

What's more, at the time I had a track record of quitting everything from baseball to karate. The real question he had was this: what made my pursuit in music any different? How could he know that this time it was the real deal? How could I guarantee him that I'd find success on this route?

From his perspective a career in music didn't guarantee any kind of financial security for my future. Even though struggle is part of any worthy journey, my dad wanted me to travel a more financially secure road. At the time it was hard for me to fully understand this because of how angry he got when expressing his concerns.

Although it scared me to travel this route towards my dreams, I don't regret my decision. With music I felt like I'd finally discovered what I wanted to do with the rest of my life. So, against my dad's wishes, I continued my pursuit of musical prosperity on my PlayStation.

> *Jumping into the beat-making process and getting my hands dirty was valuable because it helped me fail more quickly. Failure is usually something people avoid at all costs. But music taught me that failure is a prerequisite for success.*

MY FIRST BEAT

Unfortunately, due to a heavy load of homework every day, I didn't have much time to dedicate to my new love. But the few spare hours I did have I devoted to *MTV Music Generator*. I didn't spend much time going through the forty-five-page user manual. Instead I chose to dive in headfirst and only open the manual when I got stuck or had specific questions.

I found so much value in doing it this way, in jumping into the beat-making process and getting my hands dirty. Why? Because it helped me fail more quickly. Usually—and especially at that age—failure is something people avoid at all costs. But one thing that music taught me is that failure is a prerequisite for success.

One of the greatest marketing minds I've ever met is a Professor by the name of Dennis Morgan. (I first met him years later, in college.) He explained failure in much the same way. He once illustrated how commercial airplanes don't travel in straight lines to meet their destination; they purposely fly off course so that their computers update their coordinates based on how far off their flight path they are. In essence, the planes purposely *fail* so that they can better gauge how to stay on course in the future. Failure is used to their advantage.

Years before I heard the concept of failure explained so brilliantly, I was purposely flying off course every time I turned on my eighteen-inch Zenith television and PlayStation and opened up *MTV Music Generator*. I would skim through all the available sounds in the game library so I could fly off course. I sat for hours mixing and matching the kicks, snares, hi-hats, pianos, guitar riffs, basslines, and vocal samples, trying to make something I could show off to Keyden the next day.

I couldn't believe I had so many instrument choices available to me on a video game. It was like being extremely hungry and looking at a menu of forty-plus items without knowing what I wanted to eat first. The possibilities were endless. But without any clear idea of what I wanted to create I had to swallow my inner doubts and start with what came most naturally to me: the drums.

This is how it was the first time I opened the game. Sound by sound I pieced together my first drum loop. When I finished it I added one of the game's premade guitar riffs and a vocal sample that seemed to match it well. Honestly, the process felt more and more silly every time I added an instrument, but I kept going. I didn't know what the hell I was doing, but for the first time in my life, failing didn't feel like failing. It simply felt like trial and error.

Little did I know that this would be a process I would repeat for the next decade of my life.

In 2001, I doubt any library on the planet—much less my local one—had any books on how to be a PlayStation music producer. Additionally, YouTube was nowhere near as informative as it is today for music producers (and everyone else). My musical vocabulary was extremely limited, too. I didn't have any formal training in music theory and didn't know how to properly read music. So, as you can imagine, I had to teach myself a lot in those early days.

But I was up for the task. Years before I'd even thought about being a producer, I developed a love for the rhythm and percussion section in jazz bands. As a child I'd watch the drummer at my mother's church and listen to Latin jazz legends like Willie Colón and Mario Bauzá on *The Cosby Show*. I always had this deep love and appreciation for the drums. When I was younger I'd beat on the walls, making my own rhythms. I didn't know what I was doing, but it *felt right*. It was almost like a form of OCD. I'd start a beat, stop, then do it again if it wasn't perfect. And I'd repeat the process until I perfectly matched the timing of the drums I heard in my head—or until my mom told me to knock it off.

I don't remember every detail of the first beat I made or how exactly I got to the finish line. Every instrument I chose to include came from me searching for sounds I didn't even know the proper names of. It was as if all those childhood rhythms I'd pounded out on the walls were coming back to me. I wasn't going for a specific style or sound when creating my first beat. I just kept going until I felt like I couldn't come up with anything else for it. Then I exported my first *MTV Music Generator* beat to my 8 MB memory card, hoping to share it with Keyden the next day after school.

It took me almost four hours to finish that first beat on *MTV Music Generator*! But after wandering aimlessly through the dark, learning the ropes was one of the greatest feelings I'd ever experienced. It didn't matter that I didn't know exactly what I was doing. Through failure I'd learned a lot more about what I should and shouldn't do, and I had faith that those lessons would make me better. I kept reminding myself to keep going, because every beat has a humble beginning.[1]

Scan the QR code to hear an early beat.

MY FIRST FEEDBACK

When I saw Keyden the next day I couldn't shut up about how much fun I'd had and how great my first beat turned out. I've always been the type of person who gets excited about something then won't shut up about it, the guy who learns something new and feels he's got to share it with the rest of the world. If Keyden was annoyed at my enthusiasm, he didn't show it. He was used to me, and he just nodded and said he looked forward to hearing it.

---

[1] An early beat: https://youtu.be/Ssxmo9TcxqQ

At his house after school he blew the dust off his old PlayStation and handed it to me to hook up while he went to heat up a frozen burrito. I probably set a Guinness World Record that day for fastest assembly of a PlayStation. I put the game in and retrieved the memory card from my jacket pocket, then held it in the air as if that grey, 8 MB memory card contained top-secret, classified documents from the Pentagon.

Keyden laughed hysterically and said, "I can't wait to hear it, fam."

"Are you sure?" I replied. "Are you truly ready for this?"

"Yeah, man! Just play the damn beat!"

So I did. I remember being so nervous that I couldn't even look him in the eye to see his reaction. Instead I kept my own eyes glued to the television screen as it scrolled through every new section of my beat.

Three minutes and thirty seconds later the beat ended, and the room was completely silent.

When I couldn't wait anymore, I said, "So, what do you think?"

Keyden said, "It's cool, fam. You did your thing. It just sounds kind of 'video-gamey.'"

Now, even though he didn't mean "video-gamey" as a compliment, my silly, confused ass took it as one. I thought he was saying my sound selection was unique, and in a good way. I'd been heavily influenced by video game music and sounds growing up. As a kid I fell in love with the 8-bit sounds of *Metroid II: The Return of Samus*, *Tecmo Bowl*, and *The Addams Family*, courtesy of my handheld Gameboy. For those of you reading this who are too young to remember, 8-bit sounds were

Scan the QR code to hear the **Super Mario Brothers** *8-bit theme song.*

used to create a distinctive style of electronic music on vintage computers using a device called chiptune. These electronic sounds are primarily synthesized "blips." Just look up the original *Super Mario Brothers* theme song on YouTube and you'll know exactly what I'm talking about.[2]

Keyden, sensing the miscommunication, swallowed the last bite of his burrito and explained his critique. "Video-gamey," he said, wasn't quite meant as a compliment. Really it was just his initial thought upon hearing the beat. Then he said, "At the end of the day just keep going D-Weezy! If you keep at it, I think you'll start getting really good. I know you will."

I wasn't upset. I took his words to heart. They gave me all the fuel I needed to continue.

And it's good I didn't take that initial critique too harshly. In the following months, I would hear the "video-gamey" phrase used many more times, sometimes by complete strangers, to describe my beats.

On one weekend visit with my mom I showed her my first beat. Now my mom's always been one of my biggest musical supporters and influences. Aside from her own impressive taste in music, she's played the piano for over thirty-five years, so she knows a thing or two about music and music theory. I hoped that by showing her my first beat, she could shed some light on why people were describing my beats as "video-gamey."

After listening to that first beat I'd played for Keyden, she offered her own explanation. She felt that the "video-gamey" phrase was really describing the quality of the *sounds* I'd chosen to use in my beat. My drums and melodies sounded like synthetic versions of real instruments. The effect would've been completely different if the same beats were played and backed up with real instruments.

---

[2] Super Mario Brothers 8-bit theme song:
https://www.YouTube.com/watch?v=NTa6Xbzfq1U

After my mom broke it down for me like this I instantly began to hear what everybody else was hearing. My beats *did* sound video-gamey and computerized. She assured me that I'd made a good beat, but it was limited by the sounds I'd made it with.

As far as I was concerned, I thought my mother was a genius for understanding that and explaining it to me so clearly. From that day on I made it a point to start regularly consulting with her on my weekend visits.

Lessons to Take Away from Chapter 2

1. The decisions you make in your teens WILL impact the rest of your life.
2. Sometimes even the people who love you the most won't understand your dreams.
3. Seek the LOVE in the critiques your loved ones give you.
4. Failure is a checkpoint—not a destination.
5. Be open to critiques. Let them grow you—not define you.
6. Sometimes the best advice comes from the most unlikely sources.
7. Use REAL instrument sounds to create beats with REAL emotions.

CHAPTER 3

THE **KICK**

"The kick is the heartbeat of your drum loop."

~ *OSYM*

The kick is the often-unsung hero of every drum loop. It's like the Napoleon Dynamite of drum loops. What I mean by this is that many producers underestimate the value of their kicks and what they contribute to their beats. But when it comes to Hip Hop beats, my producer brother OSYM takes a unique perspective on the importance of the kick. He believes that if the kick drum is utilized correctly, it can represent the heartbeat of a drum loop.

THE INFLUENCE OF MY MOTHER

Early on in my career my mother was my kick drum.

Every producer needs the support of someone or something they consider their everything. This can be a family member, a significant other, a friend, or even a destination that keeps them going when things get rough. I know many producers will argue that a strong belief in oneself is more important, but I personally feel that this only takes you so far. My mom has and always will be my number one fan. My two younger sisters, Jazmine and Paige, and I inherited our heart, our sense of humor, our compassion for others, and our love of music from our mother.

Some of my earliest memories of my mom are of her playing the piano in church. She led the choir every Sunday at St. Peter's Rock Baptist Church in Los Angeles. It was the early 1990s, so I couldn't have been any older than five or six at the time. My mom was classically trained on piano. Growing up I saw her get invited to play at numerous churches around Los Angeles, and I was usually right there, watching her from the front row.

It was the same at choir rehearsals at St. Peter's Rock—my eyes glued to my mom as she led the choir with her right hand and played the piano keys with her left. She would often yell out commands to different sections of the choir, like:

"SOPRANOS! Okay, now ALTOS!"

I had no idea what those words meant back then, but I noticed that each time she yelled something out another section of the choir would sing. Even as a child I was mesmerized by all the sounds that burst forth when the choir sang in unison. Perhaps that's one of the reasons I use so many choir samples in my production today.

When my eyes weren't glued to my mom they would shift over to Michael on the drums. Michael was the teenage relative of a few of the members in the choir. He was talented beyond his years and had an energetic, infectious way of playing the drums. He'd often improvise every few loops with tom rolls and cymbal splashes, but he never fell off the beat. Watching him play all those years ago is probably another reason I fell in love with the sound of drums.

Many of my friends growing up asked me why my mom never taught me how to play piano. Simply put, I loved her too much to ask and she loved me too much to make me learn. As far back as I can remember, my mom worked crazy hours. When I was a little boy she worked graveyard shifts for the Huntington Park Police Department and still got up early the next morning to cook breakfast for my sisters and me. I've seen her work in high-stress environment after high-stress environment just to make sure my siblings and I had food on the plate. It was important to her that her kids had the childhood she couldn't experience. You very rarely heard her complain about having to work so much. Even through the pain of car repossessions, apartment evictions, unruly bosses, and circumstances that a woman like my mother shouldn't have to endure, she always found a reason to smile and stay faithful.

I felt guilty seeing her come home after a stressful twelve-hour work shift and two-hour choir rehearsal and still cook for me and my sisters. I felt guilty because even before I was old enough to get a job I always felt like I could contribute more. There was no way that I could ever fix up my lips to ask her to teach me the piano. I'm sure she would have gladly done it if I had, but I just couldn't bring myself to do it.

CAN I KICK IT? NO, YOU CAN'T!

I promised at the start of this book to be completely honest with you as I share my stories. I don't intend to break that promise now.

I was by no means an angel growing up. Although it was always my intention to be considerate to my mom, I still had my share of inconsiderate teenage producer moments. I think any producer who creates music in a parent's home goes through this. As an adult I try to imagine what it must have felt like to be my mom on the other side of my home studio walls. Especially in the early years! I can picture her wanting to repeatedly slam her head against a brick wall as I fumbled amateurishly through sub-heavy basslines trying to find the right key or indecisively sampled snare after snare and kick after kick. It was not an environment for the weak, or for anyone sensitive to sound. This surely wasn't something my dad was willing to put up with.

It was a catch-22 when I lived at my dad's apartment and attempted to make beats. On the one hand, I wasn't allowed to play loud music in my room because it disrupted his work. However, this was a completely reasonable complaint that a pair of headphones could solve. But on the other hand, I got disciplined if I didn't respond after he called my name a few times, regardless of whether I couldn't hear him because I had headphones on or not.

Slowly but surely I started to see that my dad's apartment wasn't going to be an environment my music could grow in. Not being able to properly hear the music I was creating made my learning experience extremely frustrating. I tried to compromise and cheat the system after school by running home as fast I could before he returned from work. I knew that if I postponed my homework until he walked in the door, I had about two hours and forty-five minutes to work on my music—loudly and without interruption. So, for several months this is what I did.

> *In those early days we were proud of the music we created with the little we had.*

When I finally graduated from high school in 2003, my dad gave me his Ford Taurus as a graduation gift. The car was mine, but under one condition: I had to go to college and get a job. I wasn't opposed to the idea at first because I knew that it was going to be a while before music could start paying my bills.

In the months prior to graduation, Keyden and I worked on dozens of songs. Many of them were produced by me, even though the beats were terrible. Keyden and I still joke today about how terrible they were. But in those early days we were proud of the music we created with the little we had. The bigger story was that we had original music and were becoming better lyricists in the process. We knew that we were getting good—just not pay-me-$5-for-this-mixtape good quite yet.

As much as school was my dad's number one priority for me, a career in music was all that I had on my mind. I desperately wanted to find a way to make a living while also making music. When I graduated from high school a part of me saw it as a golden opportunity to free up my time towards that goal. I thought I would graduate high school, work full time, and work on music on my off days. College wasn't in the plans for me because I couldn't see what it had to offer for a career in music. All I knew was that my dad had his plans for my future and I had my own.

YOU MUST GO TO COLLEGE

It was late into 2003 and I was a high-school graduate still living in my dad's apartment. I was primed and ready to start the next transition in my life, and the only thing stopping me was not having a job. After a few months of job hunting with no results, my dad asked to speak with me one night after he got home from work.

When I broke the news to him that not only had I not signed up at the local community college, but I also didn't have any plans to, he was extremely disappointed. I received the most intellectual tongue lashing I'd ever gotten from him. Keep in mind that my dad was a psychology major. He had a way with words that could make me rethink my whole life in a matter of minutes. He drilled me with questions like a seasoned attorney trained to challenge any rebuttal I could muster up.

Frankly, I had no solid answers for him as to why I didn't sign up for college—except for the fact that I had a dream I thought was worth giving all my time and energy to. So after a few more minutes of cross examination and him telling me how naïve my plan was, I caved in and signed up for classes at my local community college in Cerritos.

I tried my best to have a positive attitude about my pending college experience. But by the time I signed up, all the general education classes were full. (Cerritos Community College was notorious for being overcrowded in 2003.)

Ironically my first semester started around the same time Kanye West's album *College Dropout* became the soundtrack of my and many other rappers' and producers' lives. Kanye used to speak about his album in television interviews, explaining that the concept was deeper than just dropping out of college. He said he wasn't telling young people to drop out of college but was instead encouraging them to get the most out of their college experience, to use college to pursue their dreams instead of just getting used by the system.

I took those words to heart. If I was going to college against my will, I would make college work for me. I chose classes that I felt would best help me have a career in music instead of just random classes for units. These were the classes I chose in my first semester:

Stand Up Comedy 101 – to improve my live performance and memorization skills as a rapper

Speech Interpretation – to improve my public speaking and communication skills as a rapper

Radio & Broadcasting – to learn better vocal recording and editing techniques as a producer

World Music – to learn about different cultures and instruments from around the world as a producer

I was running an elective-class marathon. I went from dreading the time college would take away from creating music to loving what it could do for my music. I made the most out of my college experience by making it adjust to my dreams. Aside from that I

> *I went from dreading the time college would take away from creating music to loving what it could do for my music. I made the most out of my college experience by making it adjust to my dreams.*

met a lot of great people and musicians while at college. But I honestly had no intentions of earning a degree during my tenure there.

It took my dad two semesters before he caught on to my plan—and then he was even more disappointed. Back then when my dad got that angry I would usually respectfully stand down and nod in agreement with his wishes. Most times I was too afraid and intimidated to speak up for myself around him. But the older I got the more I realized that he and I saw things differently as human beings. This may be because I was gradually growing more confident about pursuing my dream.

So this time, when he started to go into cross-examination mode on me I spoke up for myself. My words came stumbling out and my thoughts were a bit scattered, but I let them out through my fear.

This only intensified his anger, and for the next few weeks it sparked disagreements so intense that I eventually chose to move in with my mom and grandparents in the middle of the semester.

Obviously this left my relationship with my dad in an odd place. But the way I saw it, I had already invested a few years in my dream and I wasn't about to stop pursuing it for anyone, even the man I respected the most. Ironically, shortly after my move to my mom's house I got offered a job at a sandwich restaurant. I accepted and clocked in the same week. Consequently, I didn't return to Cerritos

Community College for a third semester.

After I moved out and the dust settled, my dad and I eventually got back on speaking terms. One night on the phone I announced the good news about my new job. He was happy about it but more concerned about my college plans. I told him I was going to work full time while pursuing my dream in music, so college just wasn't in the cards for me. This time his reaction wasn't even anger; it was one of genuine concern.

After hanging up I didn't know how to feel about my life or my future. All I knew was that I had a new job. This meant I would finally have more consistent money coming in, and with it I knew I would be able to make major upgrades to my music equipment.

SON, I SUPPORT YOU, BUT TURN YOUR MUSIC DOWN!

Another advantage of living at my mom's (a house we shared with my grandparents) was that I had a lot more room there than I did in my dad's apartment. Specifically, there was an old patio that I set my sights on to become my official home studio. With an open space like the patio I would have nothing but time, space, volume—and the freedom to create.

The first few months at my mom's house I went beat-making crazy! I'm sure my neighbors hated my rude way of saying hello every morning: an alarm clock of 808s and synthesizers. In fact, my next-door neighbor and childhood friend, Kelen, used to text me about how dope my beats sounded from his upstairs bedroom. The only problem was that he could hear my beats loud and clear from his second story room a house away from mine!

My mom's house had been owned by my grandparents for years. The patio had thin, faux-wood walls from the 1970s. The patio looked like it might have been my grandfather's swanky man-cave. It had a vintage wooden coffee table, vintage oak wood cup coasters, and a vintage glass cigarette ashtray. When we were growing up, this patio had been a playroom for my younger sister Jazmine and me; she'd play with her dolls and I'd play Super Nintendo. The room reeked of nostalgia—and it also gave me my first taste of artistic freedom.

My mom has always supported me and my pursuit of music. She bought me my first Omega Lexicon audio interface and my first CD of drum kits. She understood what it felt like to have dreams of being successful in music, only to have those dreams denied by her parents. In fact, when my mom was younger she'd had an opportunity to be in George Clinton's legendary Parliament Funk band, but her parents weren't having it. She even had an opportunity to go to Grambling State University on a full music scholarship, but her parents didn't want her going out of state for college. So she made it a point to strongly support her children and their dreams—no matter how big or small they were.

However, even she had her limitations. I told you she worked brutal hours at her job. To make matters worse, sometimes her lack of sleep gave her intense migraines—painful headaches on steroids that make you extremely sensitive to light, smell, and sound.

The patio was directly behind my mother's bedroom. I assumed that because she worked such crazy hours and slept like a rock, I wouldn't disturb her much. Wrong. My job at the sandwich restaurant made it so I was forced to make music during the early morning hours when she was snatching a few precious hours of sleep.

I cannot possibly imagine what life was like on the other side of the patio walls. I wasn't intending to be disrespectful with the volume of my music. But my creativity was like a puppy dog that had been kept inside and never allowed to bark—and I had to let it out! The moment I got the freedom to create music as loudly as I wanted to it was like dropping that puppy off at the park where it could run wild and bark to its heart's content. I honestly didn't know how to control myself with all that freedom. I was just so happy that I finally had the chance to express myself.

Well, at least for a few months . . .

Text Message

Mom: Son, I love you. The music is sounding great. But could you turn it down please. I have a migraine.

Me: Of course, Mom, I'm sorry.

Mom: It's ok, Love You.

This was how my mom generally gave me a heads-up that she could no longer take the rattling of the walls. I loved her for this approach.

I love my mom and dad both. They obviously had two different parenting styles, but both came from a place of love. My dad grew up with a strong military upbringing and believed that discipline was best administered sternly and swiftly. And, in many ways he was correct. My mom wasn't a pushover, but she believed that she could be heard clearly without yelling. At the end of the day they both wanted me to be successful, happy, and prosperous.

That said, their approaches yielded different results. And on one particular morning, my mom's approach inspired me to go back to school.

In early 2006, on one of my off days from work, my mom came out to the patio and asked if she could talk to me for a few minutes about something important. I wasn't doing anything special except watching YouTube tutorials, so of course I said yes.

She said, "Son, I just want you to know that I'm proud of your progress and your endless pursuit of success in your music."

"Thank you, Mom!"

"When I was in Orange County today I saw these brochures for a music program in Costa Mesa that I think might interest you. From what I understand they teach you how to grow as a music producer."

"For real? I should look that up."

Not even a month later I was registered for classes at Orange Coast College in Costa Mesa, California. In retrospect, I see that life's not always about what you're saying so much as how you say it. On paper my mom and dad were saying the same thing, but their approaches made all the difference.

The ironic thing is that understanding this communication skill came in handy when I began to sell beats years later. But we'll talk about that later in the book.

OH, NOW HE WANTS TO GO TO COLLEGE?!

Even before my mom came into my studio that morning I was actually beginning to miss my time at college. Those first two semesters at Cerritos Community College taught me a lot and gave me many opportunities to network with new musicians. But to be honest, I don't think I would have gone back to school had my mom not suggested it.

> *It's not always about what you're saying so much as how you're saying it. Your approach makes all the difference.*

When I first set foot on the beautiful Orange Coast College campus I quickly realized my experience would be different from the one I'd had at CCC. Something felt dramatically different this go around. For starters, OCC was nowhere near as congested as Cerritos College, probably because it had a much larger campus. Additionally, OCC was only a few miles away from Newport Beach. Because of this, the school was a de facto beach community of super chill surfers, beach bums, and modern day hippies who got good grades in their spare time.

Now that may be an over-exaggerated, blanket generalization of OCC's student demographic, but my point is that things here were different from anything else I'd encountered. I attended that semester with plans to join their music production and audio engineering program. But when I went to sign up those classes were full. I would have to wait to take them until the next semester, and in the meantime I needed to find other classes to occupy my time.

At first this discouraged me, but I reminded myself about the promise I'd made to my mom and myself. In my second go around there was no way I would leave that campus without some sort of document representing completion. I promised myself that I'd dedicate my focus and time at college with the same intensity I'd used making beats on *MTV Music Generator*.

With that in mind, my first-semester classes looked like this:

Principles of Advertising – to learn how to promote myself online, specifically with Myspace

Improv Comedy – to learn how to be more comfortable onstage as a rapper

Introduction to Small Business – to learn the basics of running my own business

> *I promised myself that I'd dedicate my focus and time at college with the same intensity I'd used making beats on MTV Music Generator.*

These classes made the hour-long drive from my mom's house in Carson well worth the commute. To balance both work and school I had to request that I take fewer hours at my day job; at the time I was working well over forty hours a week. My boss wasn't happy about my request because I had recently been promoted to Night Shift Manager. Without me around as much he would have to hire more people.

He tried numerous times to convince me to quit school and go to Sandwich University instead. Yes, Sandwich University. I kindly declined. I felt it was irresponsible of him to do that, and it made me angry. He had a way of being patronizing when acting curious about what my major might be. When I finally told him it was music-related he couldn't help but laugh. There was a positive to this: his laughter filled me with fury and determination. I told myself that I HAD to complete something so I would never again in my life have to work a job like that.

THE MOST BRILLIANT MARKETING MIND I'VE EVER MET

Costa Mesa was significantly more chill than Carson, and school started becoming my healthy escape. In 2006, Carson wasn't necessarily the worst place to live, but because it was sandwiched between the worst parts of Compton and Long Beach it had its share of gangs and violent crimes. Even when I was in Curtiss Middle School (from which I took the first part of my producer name) there was a constant background stress you had to learn to live with in Carson. Even the teachers were subject to this stress and fear, and it affected the way they taught us. Thankfully at OCC you didn't have to deal with these kinds of concerns. The teachers at OCC treated their students with respect, but also expected more of them.

Of all my first semester classes at OCC, the one that made the biggest impact on me was Principles of Advertising. It was here I met one of the most influential and brilliant marketing minds in my life: Professor Dennis Morgan.

Professor Morgan was a tall, middle-aged white guy with glasses and a small grey ponytail. He spoke in a stern, authoritative, and sincere tone. He constantly reminded us how marketing was his number one passion—not because of the money it made him, but because of the opportunity it gave him to help others. He was unlike any professor I've had before or since. He had a skill for breaking down the most complex topics in marketing into simple and easily digestible examples. His lectures were like TED talks. There was never a dull moment in his classroom.

The first day he covered his curriculum and what he expected from us as students in his class. Before we left that day he made a proposal to us. He explained that he had a special message he wanted to give to only those of us interested in receiving it. He claimed that this message would be *the most valuable lesson he could ever teach us* if we chose to stay and listen. The catch was that he would only tell us this lesson once and never bring it up again.

Now, mind you, this was the last class of the day. It ended at 9:30 p.m., when most of us were ready to go home and sleep. I was especially ready to go because I knew I had an hour-long drive ahead of me. However, something told me to stay that night. After several students left, Professor Morgan closed the door and delivered a fifteen-minute message about the importance of attitude in life.

In this message, he explained how our ATTITUDE ultimately determines our ALTITUDE in our career and life. He emphasized that our future success will always be predicated upon the attitude we choose to have about life. And no matter what line of business we choose to go into, if we don't believe in our hearts that it can help people, we should not pursue it, because ultimately we will not get the results we truly desire to see.

> *Your ATTITUDE ultimately determines your ALTITUDE in your career and life.*

It was one of those speeches you only see in the movies. You could tell it was delivered from a sincere place in his heart. Most importantly, it was delivered from the mind of an accomplished man who had mentored some of Hollywood's biggest entertainers. It sprang from the experience of someone who had achieved great success and who was now driven to teach young men and women how to be the greatest versions of themselves through marketing and advertising.

After his speech, I drove home in complete silence. I was beyond inspired. He was the first person I had ever heard describe business as an art form. He was also the first person I had ever heard make a legitimate argument about success in business being directly correlated with being a good human being. I felt like I had been lied to all my life by being told that me being a good guy was the reason I wouldn't succeed in the music business. I obviously had a pretty naïve view of the world of business, but I was eager to make a change.

MY X-FACTOR

This is the foundation of my success as a Prosperous Producer. The attitude you choose to adopt and exhibit is the X-Factor separating you from your potential success as a producer. It's not about the equipment or the opportunities that you don't have. It's all about how you view what you DO have. Producers, I don't have any cheat codes, shortcuts, or secrets on how to make it in the music business. And anyway, I don't personally believe in secrets being the answer to your problems. Every success I've had came out of four personal commitments I chose to make: work hard, remain patient, stay consistent, and make time to grow. (And, okay, maybe there was some luck along the way, too, but I had to be prepared to take advantage of it.)

I have over fourteen years of trial and error experience that I hope can cut in half the time it takes you to succeed. I have placements, awards, and other achievements that I plan to share with you in this book. But that's only half of my story.

I'm not here to sell you on anything except yourself. If you want to know what drives me daily, THESE are the stories I mix into every beat I create. The prosperity I have attained today as a music producer is not just rooted in how well I learned *MTV Music Generator*. My prosperity is not just rooted in all the tips and tricks I picked up from legends along the way. My prosperity is not just rooted in what I learned in school or in the beat-leasing business. My prosperity has been driven by my mindset, my work ethic, and my heart.

> *Every success I've had came out of four personal commitments I chose to make: work hard, remain patient, stay consistent, and make time to grow.*

THIS BOOK

So let me just take a break from the story here and make something clear. My goal with this book is to bring you a perspective that often gets overlooked in many music industry-related books. I refuse to lie to you. I want you to understand that my road was a difficult one through trials, tribulations, and triumphant wins. It is a miracle that I am typing these words to you right now. I wasn't supposed to be here. I am enormously grateful that I get to wake up every day and make beats for a living. I make good money at it and I believe you can too.

This book covers many practical strategies I've never shared before. But its true value is the window into the mindset I adopted on my journey, because that's what was required to get me to where I am today.

You can create the same mindset within yourself.

So, if you're ready, let's continue.

Lessons to Take Away from Chapter 3

1. Sometimes it's not about what you're saying, but how you say it.
2. Everyone needs a support system in their early stages.
3. Be flexible to change.
4. Your attitude will ultimately determine your altitude in this—or any—business.

CHAPTER 4

THE **SWING**

"Without Swing, you have Restriction,
With Restriction you have no Freedom.
Without Freedom there is no Soul."

~ *Captain (Producer)*

If the kick is the heartbeat of a drum loop then the swing of a beat is its *soul*. The swing gives us a precious reminder that a human being laid hands to the creation of a beat. The act of swinging an instrument off the grid, of freeing it from the mechanical timing of a metronome, gives the illusion that it was recorded live and was subject to natural human error. The swing evokes an attitude that is the *secret sauce* of many of your favorite beats.

Trying to explain swing to a producer who has no idea what you're talking about is like a woman trying to describe the pains of childbirth to a man. It took me years to understand what swing was and why it was SO significant to my beats. Recently, I uploaded a meme on my Facebook about the difficulty producers have in understanding swing—and chaos ensued. My comment section filled up with arguments between hardware and software producers about the true definition of swing.

Needless to say, this is a very touchy and confusing subject for many, but here we go.

Legendary jazz bassist Charles Mingus once described swing as a tempo that's never a straight line but which, in its truest essence, *suggests* that straight line. Take, for example, a professional drummer. If you record this drummer playing endless loops of the same rhythm, no matter what your ears *hear*, that drummer isn't playing in perfect time. It might be close—in fact, it

> **The swing gives us an inside look at the attitude that inspired the music.**

should be close enough to keep everyone else in time—but it's not *perfect*. Humans are not designed to play with the same mundane accuracy of a robot. It's their *swing* that gives soul and life to the music. The swing gives us an inside look at the attitude that inspired the music.

In Hip Hop, the swing of a beat is EVERYTHING.

CRITIQUING MY BEATS

In 2004 I started getting comfortable making beats. I also finally got past my peers calling my beats "video-gamey" and began developing a long list of my own personal critiques of my beats. During my analysis, I made the all too common producer mistake of comparing my beats to those made by veteran producers too early in my process. Although it pushed me to become better faster, I often found that going this route made me feel like I was always doing things the wrong way. My expectations were unrealistic, because at this stage in my career I lacked some basic knowledge of the field of producing. Comparing myself to other producers this early caused me to develop an inferiority complex.

This was most evident when I compared my drums to theirs. Don't get me wrong: my drums have always been my biggest strength. But back in those days there was something missing that I couldn't quite put my finger on. Years later I would come to understand that my beats were missing the all-important swing. The rhythms of my beats sounded too robotic and I didn't know why.

> **Learn from the best, but don't compare yourself to them early on.**

There were producers who early on tried to tell me I was too much on the grid, but I wasn't sure how to fix that without sabotaging the beat.

In retrospect, I know exactly why I couldn't hear what they heard. As time passed I eventually learned that swing isn't something you see with your eyes, or even really hear. Swing is something you have to FEEL in your heart.

HOW I FOUND MY SOUND AS A PRODUCER

One of my greatest production mentors came into my life in 2006 in the form of TDE producer Tae Beast. Tae has been responsible for the production of some of Kendrick Lamar's and Ab-Soul's most popular songs. I had the pleasure of being mentored by Tae years before those credits, when he was the co-founder of an Inglewood-based independent label I was signed to called Rocstarr Ent.

I was floored the first time I heard a beat by Tae Beast. He was the first producer I'd heard who told an in-depth story with his music before the lyrics were added. Everything from his sample choices, his song structure, and his instrument placement spoke to me. His beats evoked real emotions in his listeners. They didn't sound like a monotonous loop; they sounded like legit scores to award-winning independent films at the Sundance Festival. In much the same way you can identify a warm meal cooked with love, you could tell that love was a prime ingredient in his music.

I, on the other hand, just made *tight beats*. My beats weren't at the level where they were bleeding with my passion and personality. But simply observing Tae in his zone led me to believe that SOUL was the missing ingredient in my music. I thought that by filling that void in my production I would have the answer to the robotic quality of my compositions.

> *Tae did what any great mentor is supposed to do: he gave just enough information to point me in the right direction. If I remained hungry for an answer, I would end up not only SEEING but FEELING the solution for myself.*

In simpler terms, I really wanted to find my own sound as a producer. Tae had his own sound and it made me want to pick his brain every chance I got. When I asked him questions on the topic he wouldn't flat out tell me the answers. Tae purposely made me think long and hard about what those answers might be. He knew the exact answers to my questions. But he did what any great mentor is supposed to do: he gave just enough information to point me in the right direction. If I remained hungry for an answer, that direction would not only lead me to SEEING the solution but also to FEELING it for myself.

Tae used to give me producer homework assignments. At his direction, I compiled a list of my top five favorite Hip Hop beats of all time. Next, I was instructed to loop the drums on all five beats and drag them into my beat-making program. Then I was to copy every element that I could hear in that drum loop, mute the original loop, and then play my newly created drum loop and try to FEEL the difference. As soon as I felt the difference, I was then told to remove the sounds I didn't personally like and replace them with new sounds. Lastly, I was told to manually shift the timing of any instrument that didn't feel on time with the original loop.

This process, though tedious, was a game-changer for me. By paying that much attention to just the timing of the drums in my favorite beats, I was able see and feel what I couldn't before. This was the first time that I felt the swing of a beat. This is when I learned that the swing of a beat lies in the subtle placement and misplacement of instruments. Simultaneously, the process changed my opinion of a lot of my favorite beats. It actually made me dislike certain elements in them. For example, the more I did this process, the more I looked past how much I LOVED producer Just Blaze's kick and snare combinations and the more I focused on how much I disliked his style of hi-hats. It wasn't necessarily that his hi-hat rhythms were bad; it simply wasn't the style I preferred. I found that I preferred the hi-hat rhythms of southern producers like DJ Toomp.

So maybe the most important thing this process did was take those favorite beats off my personal pedestal. Tae was a genius for suggesting this because it demystified these classic beats. I did this homework assignment at least once a day for a year, and along the way I learned so much about myself as a producer.

One of the most practical lessons I learned, the one that gave me my first introduction to the DNA of swing, was that by manually placing the snare slightly early and late in certain sections of my beats I created a more natural, live feel to the sound.

SWING SHIFTS AT THE SANDWICH JOB

The music industry is much like life itself: full of valleys and peaks. This is just part of the human experience we sign up for when we're born. For many of us in pursuit of our dreams, a 9-5 is a necessary valley before we reach our musical peaks. My own valley lasted for four years when I was employed by a local sandwich restaurant. Of all the lessons I learned over the years en route to becoming a Prosperous Producer, no experience taught me more than that job. For one thing, it made me never want another one like it in my life.

When I received my first placement with Kendrick Lamar and Ab-Soul back in the mid-2000s, you know how I celebrated it? By clocking in at work and having an argument with a difficult customer about whether or not he ordered tomatoes on his chicken sandwich.

If there was any place that should've taught me about the art of SWING, it was there. Just the smell of prime rib and carbonara sauce on my apron every night gave me *mood* swings. Ironically, I worked the swing shift, aka, the shift where you have the glorious duties of cleaning up after the morning shift AND handling irritable customers while understaffed.

Now, I don't want to give you the impression that I was ungrateful about having a job. I searched long and hard for one, so finally having a job was an absolute blessing. Anything that gave me a chance to help out my mom and to pay for my music equipment, car loan and occasional dates with pretty women was well worth the sacrifice. I was finally getting consistent checks that my music wasn't providing.

But that blessing slowly transformed into a bigger and bigger nuisance as the owner started to become horribly irresponsible.

What went wrong? Well, for example, we were supposed to get paid on Fridays. But if the owner didn't report his numbers to corporate on time, our checks would come in late. When this happened our regular checks were temporarily replaced with personal checks which we weren't allowed to cash until Monday. When you're living paycheck to paycheck, like most of us were, waiting all weekend to get some money in your pocket is, to put it mildly, challenging.

Wait, there's more.

Sometimes the air conditioner went down, making it extremely uncomfortable to work behind the counter. After this had been going on for a while the owner admitted that he would turn it off himself, lock down the controller and then tell us the unit was malfunctioning. It was just a tactic he used to cut his business expenses.

The icing on the cake was his state-of-the-art surveillance system, which pointed more cameras at his employees than his customers. He would literally watch my shift from his laptop surveillance system at home and call in instructions—instructions that often kept us at work hours after we had clocked out and stopped getting paid.

There were times when I absolutely hated that job. The only highlights were laughing with my co-workers and working with battle rap legend Daylyt (before the face tattoos). Outside of work it was no secret to anyone around me that the job was taking a toll on me. Often after working twelve-hour shifts I had little to no time or energy to work on music. My sandwich job was slowly but surely taking away from the very dream I needed it to support.

Things got a little better after my third year there. I was promoted to night shift manager, and being in that position allowed me to hire some of my music friends onto the staff. To this day I doubt the individuals I hired have any idea how much their presence helped me keep my sanity at that job.

Still—that job was the ultimate pain in the ass. Even though I had reason to appreciate it, it was a big source of my unhappiness in life at the time. Like most disgruntled employees, the problems of my job always seemed to follow me home somehow—it seemed like I could never actually clock out. Those problems even accompanied me to the studio, like when my collaborators would ask why I looked so exhausted.

MOOD SWINGS: ARE YOU HAPPY OR NAH?

One of my favorite motivational speakers, Tony Robbins, often talks about the power of fulfillment. He says that as human beings we're wired to believe that achievement is a bigger priority than our need to be happy and fulfilled. And even though that job didn't make me happy in and of itself, it was a necessary step on my path to achievement.

Most of the time it brought out the worst in me. But there were times it did the opposite. Dealing with the drama in that environment made me look at the popular cliché of "taking the good with the bad" in a whole new light. With that job I was finally making money to help support my family and my dreams, yet I still wasn't happy.

When you make the decision to be happy in life, you'll probably realize pretty quickly that it's a full-time job. It requires constant focus and action. Happiness is directly related to gratitude for a good reason. When you're grateful for the good *and* the bad things that happen to you, nobody can steal your happiness away. Just think about it for a second: can we truly give credit to all the good things that happen to us without the contribution of those who have done us wrong? Would I be as motivated as I am to GIVE, had I not experienced the pain of loss? It's important in our pursuit of being Prosperous Producers that we examine this concept, and examine it often. Ask yourself, who in your life deserves forgiveness? What stories have you been telling yourself and others about the most painful of experiences in your life? Do those stories ultimately help or continue to hurt you?

> **What stories have you been telling yourself and others about the most painful of experiences in your life? Do those stories ultimately help or continue to hurt you?**

However, before I could fully understand this concept I had to be honest with my feelings about my job. I was angry because I felt like the time I spent there could have been better spent making music. But the harsh reality was that my dreams weren't paying my bills. My job was. And some of the money I made was paying for the gear I needed to *make* that music.

There were other things to consider. For example: Yes, I was only making $8.00 an hour, but the average human being in the world survives off far less money. Yes, the AC got turned off on purpose, and it was unfair and irresponsible, but as a result fewer customers came in. This meant less work: the fewer the customers, the less we had to clean up at the end of the night.

This zone of optimistic thinking caused a ripple effect in my mentality that lasts even to this day. The way I see it, it's imperative for your success and mental wellbeing to do your absolute best to find the good in every situation.

If you're a producer currently holding down a job you don't like, I challenge you to find happiness where you stand. Don't just bask in happiness when you finally get back to working on your music. Learn to love the things you hate but know you have to do to be successful. Tony Robbins also says that life happens *for* us and not *to* us, and I truly believe that. Learn to love your life not just when things are looking up, but right now, in the belly of the beast. Find love smack in the middle of a job you absolutely hate. Be thankful for the small things like your big toe—without it you wouldn't be able to keep your balance when walking. If your legs don't work, be thankful for the man who created the wheelchair. If you can't afford a wheelchair, be thankful you've been blessed with another day to work toward making things better in your life. This change in thinking will give your life the extra boost of daily energy required to take the good with the bad while pursing your dreams.

> **Learn to love your life not just when things are looking up, but right now, in the belly of the beast.**

THE *CAPTAIN* OF SWING

Have you ever met somebody who's annoyingly AMAZING at *EVERYTHING*?

I'm not talking about just better-than-the-average-human-being amazing either.

I'm talking about born-to-do-whatever-he-sets-his-sights-on amazing.

I know somebody like that and he goes by the producer name of Captain. In the time since I met him he's gone from being a sponsored skater to a trendsetting producer and all the way to his present-day profession as a mixed martial arts fighter.

Now because my interactions with Captain are so important to how I understand the concept of swing, I'm going to jump a few years ahead in my personal story and tell you more about him.

Captain was the first producer to ever extensively explain to me the concept of swing and how it works. He used to say that every producer has their own swing, and the only way to find it is to feel for it.

Captain was also the first producer I met who paid as much attention to the details of his drums as I did to my own. Part of the reason I love producing Hip Hop beats so much is because in our culture we always find cool ways to break the traditional rules of creating music. I used to take full advantage of Hip Hop being a genre that was unafraid to flirt with the red levels on the volume meter; I used music-mixing terms like "distortion" and "peaking" unashamedly when describing my beats. In my book those were alternative terms used to describe how much my beats SLAPPED!

However, everything I thought I knew about the art of beat *slappage* slowly went out the window the day I met Captain during one of my first beat battles in Riverside.

In 2009 I moved out to the Inland Empire in Southern California. I kept hearing about Captain from multiple residents in the area. People described his beats as having some of the heaviest drums they'd ever heard. I found out later they were inspired by his days as a Krump dancer. The eclectic rhythms in Krump dancing inspired him to structure and manipulate his beats in unorthodox ways. That said, he didn't look at his beats as unorthodox; he just felt they had a different swing than those of most other producers.

The Kill That Noise (KTN) beat battle—hosted by Inland Empire-based promotion company Bricktoyaface—used to bring out the best producers that the Inland Empire had to offer. It certainly brought out the best in me as a producer when I competed. For those producers out there who have never competed in a beat battle, there is no better test of your belief in your music and decision-making skills under pressure than when you compete in one.[3]

Before I went head-to-head with Captain I did my research on him. Other producers in the city were telling me he was the guy to worry about most if I chose to jump into the KTN beat battle. But even if I hadn't done any research, I would've realized this the moment he played his first beat against me.

Captain's beat started off with a very misleading and simplistic

---

[3] I also write more about beat battles in Chapter 10.

8-bit melody line. Oh, the irony. After the melody line repeated two times, the most disrespectful, in-your-face drums came raging in. (His snares came through so crisp on his beats that I used to joke with him that I could smell the wood breaking off the drummer's sticks through the speakers.) His hi-hats were unpredictable in that they would be completely on beat one minute and completely off beat in other sections.

I was amazed by it all, but the thing that stood out to me the most was his swing. My lessons with Tae Beast had taught me about swing slowly but steadily. But Captain's beats that night had an immediate impact. They gave an extremely clear *feel* of what swing was and how it had the ability to affect the emotion a beat conveyed to its listener.

> **"Every producer has their own swing, and the only way to find it is to feel for it."**
> **~ Captain**

Captain's history as a Krump dancer also made him a natural entertainer in his beat battles. He was the first producer I'd ever seen physically express the movement of certain instruments in his beat. He knew his beats so well that he never missed a mute, drop, breakdown, or cue with his movements. While most producers would just stand around and nod their heads during their battles, Captain would physically act out his hi-hat rolls with his fingers or stomp his feet in time with his kick drums. His showmanship made crowds go wild.

Even before it was over I was all but sure I'd lost my battle to Captain that night. All I had were my on-the-grid soul sample beats. They weren't really what you'd consider "beat-battle" beats, though they *were* heavy. The first one I played against Captain received a lukewarm response, probably because he'd already stolen the show with his dancing. It didn't help that I just sat there with my arms nervously crossed as my first beat played.

When he played his second beat I thought my fate was sealed even further. He stepped up his performance yet another notch by throwing his hat into the crowd and dancing with the excited onlookers.

In a last-ditch, what-the-hell-do-I-have-to-lose effort I played the best beat I had left. It had a sample from David Ruffin's classic song "Love Has Gone." Now *that* got an immediate and loud reaction from the audience and the beat-battle judges. And Captain's dancing had inspired me to get out of my nervous shell and start acting out my beat as well. The more I did so, the louder the audience got. The judges even started getting out of their seats.

When all was said and done, I had somehow pulled off an upset victory over Captain.[4]

After that battle, Captain and I went from strangers to friends to arch enemies to friends to arch enemies— and eventually to being lifelong brothers. Over the years we found we had a lot in common, including the fact that we both used a computer program called FruityLoops. We began working so much together that we had a short stint where we were a production duo called GOTTEM COACH. In our collaboration sessions we specifically taught each other techniques on FruityLoops.

Scan the QR code to view the Captain vs. Curtiss Beat Battle.

COULD YOU POSSIBLY MENTOR ME?

Producers are weird.

Well, at least the good ones are. We're from another planet. We

---

[4] Captain vs. Curtiss Beat Battle: https://youtu.be/UsW9igUUD4M

speak in parametric parables and reverberating riddles. As both rapper and producer, I see it from both sides of the coin. Rappers generally see producers as weirdos and hermits—and I don't think their analysis is far off. I've been blessed to meet all kinds of producers in my career. And no matter how famous or unknown they happen to be, they're all weird in their own way.

I too have my weirdo tendencies, but I embrace them fully. As producers, our lifestyles are much more low key than rappers. We spend countless hours in front of our computers trying our best to perfect the mix on our snares. Our job makes it so we don't need to have a whole lot of human interaction. We're not required to pop bottles for club events, and when most of us do show up to places like this we're like fish out of water. Thanks to the Internet and email, sometimes we don't even have to be in the studio with the people we're producing. I'm willing to bet that a lot of producers would never experience sunlight if we didn't have to do silly things like EAT and go to WORK to SURVIVE. What's our typical idea of fun? Installing brand new VSTs and drum kits.

> *It felt like almost every producer I approached for advice told me either "Tough luck" or gave me a clichéd, canned response like, "Keep going!" Their indifference made me feel alone and without direction in the industry.*

But it's my belief we were made to be different, and most of us embrace that difference. Outcasts in life usually find comfort confiding in other outcasts. They travel in packs—wolves with other wolves, and so on. But for some unfortunate reason this hasn't always been the case for music producers in Hip Hop. When I finally had the balls to share my beats with other producers, they went out of their way to express their disapproval with them. I remember receiving a lot of backhanded compliments, things like, "Your beat is cool. It's actually not all the way wack for a beat made on a PlayStation."

Well, that was rude. I tried my best to take these critiques as constructive criticisms and not personal attacks. I understood early on that the only way to grow was to get honest feedback. But when I asked for tips . . .

Me: "Do you have any suggestions on how I can improve?"

Producer: "Nope. Nobody taught me, so you're on your own bro."

> *I promised myself that if I ever got into a position of power and influence I wouldn't use my position to talk down to my peers. I would share my value through teaching my community.*

It felt like almost every producer I approached for advice told me either "Tough luck" or gave me a clichéd, canned response like, "Keep going!" Their indifference made me feel alone and without direction in the industry. One part of me wanted to keep asking around, hoping that someone would be so gracious as to drop an actual gem on me. However, the other part of me was feeling a growing animosity towards them for not being willing to help me. That animosity made me want to prove to them that I could learn my own way—without them.

Neither the hope nor the animosity would last long. I'd often refer back to the lesson I learned from Professor Morgan about attitude and altitude. When I reminded myself of that talk it brought me comfort and helped me center myself again. When I refocused I started to view the disapproval and indifference of these other producers as blessings in disguise. Their attitude made me promise myself that if I ever got into a position of power and influence I wouldn't use my position to talk down to my peers. I told myself that if I ever achieved enough success to be your favorite producer's favorite producer, I wouldn't act like them. If I ever reached a level of value like that, I would share it through teaching my community.

BE LIKE MARTHA STEWART

In 2010 the industry was full of producers like this. They'd hold on to their secrets like their careers depended on it.

Captain's approach was the complete opposite and, as it turned out, so was mine. Captain wasn't afraid to share his knowledge and techniques; it made him feel powerful, valuable, and helpful. And I was the same. I never had reservations about sharing my so-called "secrets" with any of the producers I worked with. I always felt like no matter what information a producer took from me, there was no

> *Sharing your secrets makes you more valuable to your audience.*

way it could hurt me. I believed that if my intentions were pure, my karma was sure to be positive as well. Even if a particular producer intended to steal my "secrets," if he didn't personally understand why I utilized certain techniques or how and when to properly employ them, it wouldn't hurt me no matter what he did with them. I never quite understood the philosophy that so many producers share when it comes to being private about their secret beat-making recipes. I always felt that mindset was driven by ego and insecurity.

I like to use the example set by a certain television chef to further illustrate this point. Martha Stewart is one of the most popular chefs and brands in the world today. Yet she shares every single recipe she creates—and she cooks it right in front of our eyes. She even provides the opportunity to purchase the exact pots, pans, and spatulas she uses to cook with. Martha literally gives her viewers every tool they need to be their own version of Martha Stewart at home. She withholds no secrets and she also doesn't send you on any unnecessary wild goose chases. All she's concerned with is giving you her value.

So why doesn't she worry about having her recipes stolen from her? My answer: Martha understands the basic principles of providing value. She knows that by sharing her secrets it doesn't make her less valuable, but rather significantly more valuable to her audience. She knows you and I can take her best fried chicken recipe, use her pots, and open a restaurant right next door to her and call it Stewena Marthena. But she's not worried. She knows you still won't have the power to put her out of business. Why not? Because by sharing her value on a consistent basis it makes her too valuable to her audience to be replaced by a new opportunist.

I continue to learn so much from my friend Captain about the invisible barriers we set in our minds as human beings. He inspires me daily with the thought that we can achieve anything we want when we set the bar high enough and push ourselves to leap over it. Captain was ahead of his time when I met him in 2009. Nowadays, the same producers who used to poke fun at his beat swing and onstage dancing are attempting to do the same exact thing. Go figure.

Lessons to Take Away from Chapter 4

1. The swing provides the soul to your beats.
2. The swing isn't something you see—it's something you feel.
3. Learn from the best! But don't compare your early efforts at beat making with the best efforts of top producers with more experience and better equipment. Everyone's got to start somewhere.
4. Every producer has his or her own swing, and if you keep at it you'll find yours.
5. Learn to love the things you hate but must do to succeed.
6. Sharing your value creates abundance, not scarcity.

CHAPTER 5

THE **HI-HATS**

"The Hi-Hats provide a beat a very special illusion."

~ *Sallis*

Producers: hi-hats are the unsung heroes in our beats. A mentor of mine named Sallis used to say that hi-hats give a *special illusion* of the true speed of a beat. Ain't that the truth?

Think about your favorite trap beat.[5] Compare the energy of the first part of that beat without hi-hats to the 8-bar mark when the hi-hats make their appearance. Don't you notice a shift in the momentum? Most

Scan the QR code to learn more about trap beats.

---

[5] https://en.wikipedia.org/wiki/Trap_music

listeners haven't the slightest clue why, but producers know how much the simple addition of hi-hats can create a shift in energy. Whether it's the rapid fire hi-hats of producer Sonny Digital or the unpredictable hi-hat rolls of Metro Boomin, the hi-hats give the story of your beat some much needed momentum. Hi-hats are the Gorilla Glue that keeps the energy of your beat intact. They're like unpredictable slot machines; they keep us on the edge of our seats.

EQUIPMENT UPGRADES

Let's rewind from 2010 back to when I started receiving consistent paychecks at my sandwich job in 2004. By then I was a few years deep into making beats. Outside of my work with Keyden I didn't collaborate with many artists or producers. Together he and I filled up a shoebox with cassettes containing songs we recorded in his room over my beats. With each cassette, you heard a dramatic improvement not just in our songwriting capabilities but also in my production skills.

> *Just as we buy new shoes when our feet outgrow them, I bought new equipment when as a producer I outgrew my existing equipment.*

The improvement in my production was a result of hard work, persistence, and some major studio equipment upgrades. Now, I don't want to mislead any aspiring producers into believing that my studio upgrades were the sole reason that my beats improved. That may have been part of it, but I think the true source of my growth was my relentless effort to master the equipment I already had. Just as we buy new shoes when our feet outgrow them, I bought new equipment when as a producer I outgrew my existing equipment.

Thanks to my job I was able to afford the necessary upgrades. My

PlayStation 1 was starting to malfunction so I saved up and purchased a PlayStation 2. Also, after some research on the Internet I learned about a method that would allow me to *cleanly* transfer the music I was creating from my PlayStation to my computer. I emphasize "cleanly" because prior to that my method of getting my music from my PS1 to my computer was a bit barbaric. I would use my $15 RadioShack headset microphone to record the beat directly out of my television speakers onto my desktop computer. As you can imagine the quality was horrendous. The Zenith television I made beats on was old and didn't carry a strong bass signal. Thus, most of my beats had absolutely no low end and were painfully high pitched.

However, thanks to an article I found online at *PC World*, I learned about a desktop computer soundcard at Fry's Electronics that would allow me to record sounds directly from my PlayStation to my computer using RCA cables. Ironically, as I made these equipment upgrades, *MTV Music Generator* chose to release an updated version of their game for the PS2. I bought it the first day it came out. A few weeks later I blew another one of my sandwich job paychecks on surround sound speakers I found at Walmart. With those speakers I felt like I could finally hear my beats the way I intended them to be heard.

I noticed that every time I made a necessary upgrade I could catch more and more flaws within my music. The more flaws I found and corrected, the better I became.

YOU GOTTA KEEP IT REAL

As I became a better producer I also became a more experimental rapper. From the very beginning of my rap career I made it pretty evident that I wanted to live life outside the box. My desire to push past boundaries as a rapper was mostly attributable to the fact that I was a HUGE Outkast fan. Andre 3000 was and still is my favorite rapper of all time. What I loved most about Outkast's music was the connection I felt to the freedom they expressed. I wanted that same freedom to come through in my own music. I wanted to make crazy eclectic beats and sing like Andre 3000 did on *The Love Below*. My newfound freedom was changing me creatively and making me an even more eclectic weirdo of a human being.

At this point I was still in Soulja Camp with Keyden, but every time I went to visit him it was becoming more and more evident to both of us that we were heading in different creative directions. Keyden was a lyricist in the purest form and I was turning into an out-of-tune singer who wanted to make funk rap songs. I was spending a *lot* of time by myself on that patio in Carson. I was trying out new stuff with my voice that I'd heard in the George Clinton songs I grew up listening to. I was testing out high notes that I would've been WAY too embarrassed to do in front of my big brother. During this highly experimental phase I started working on a solo album called *You Gotta Keep It Real.* The project was entirely produced by me. I didn't really have a specific creative direction to go in but it felt good to just be weird and have fun. And I think that having worked on my own material as an artist helps me understand that side of the equation when I'm producing other rappers.

Keyden—encouraging older brother that he was—always supported my new direction even when he didn't understand it. And regardless of our new creative differences, Keyden and I tried our best to make it work out as a group. But we eventually decided to call it quits as a duo. There were no hard feelings. It was a decision we made with our brotherhood and motto in mind: ***DO IT FOR THE FAM.***

THE POWER OF COLLABORATION

After Keyden and I met at his apartment to discuss our decision to do our own music I returned to my lonely studio in Carson and continued creating. Although it hurt that my brother and I weren't an official duo anymore, I was happy to be back at my mom's house making music. I was also happy to be living in my childhood city of Carson. This was the same city where I'd played Little League baseball at Del Amo Park and attended elementary and middle school.

Since I had so much history invested in Carson, I also had the opportunity to spend more time with a few childhood friends who still lived there. One of these was my middle school buddy, John.

John and I had actually reconnected a few years before I moved back to Carson, when I still lived with my dad in Downey. John had always been an avid listener to—and walking database of—soul music. Over the years he developed into a very skilled piano player. He used to invite me to his house to play me the music he'd been working on.

When life got hectic for me in those days, John's house was a place to escape to. He had a live drum set, recording equipment, a Triton keyboard and a brain full of creative ideas. I would show him my newest beats and he would give me honest feedback on how I could improve them. It was the first time any other producer was willing to do that for me. I made sure to return the favor when he played me his own beats. Before we knew it our impromptu listening sessions turned into impromptu studio sessions.

John was big on using live instrumentation in our music. He introduced me to the magic of recording sounds without using a metronome as my guide. His process was completely different from mine. Instead of choosing from a library of video game sounds, John would pick from individual sounds pre-recorded on his Triton keyboard and play them live directly into his computer. Instrument by instrument he would record his kicks, snares, hi-hats, percussion and melodies into his multitrack recording program. He would usually start his beat off with drums to establish the swing and groove. Next he would use his mouse to highlight the loop points where he thought his drums sounded the best. Seeing him work with such flexibility and accuracy was part of the reason I stopped making beats on my PlayStation.

> *John showed me how the inflections and tones I chose for my beats could contradict the message of the lyrics and melody of my music. I gave him a sense of the importance of spacing instruments during the mix so that every sound gets its opportunity to shine.*

The more familiar I became with John's process, the more we began working on songs and eventually projects together. John taught me what it truly meant to be a producer and not just a beat maker. He provided me a point of view as a producer that I didn't have when I was Curtiss King the rapper.

Many times, artists are so married to the process of creating music that they lose out on the perspective of their audience. I was no different. It was easy for me to spend hours focusing on ways to make my rap lyrics more clever with abstract punchlines and entertaining sound effects. But at the same time it was just as easy for me to completely miss the fact that 90 percent of my audience wouldn't care how clever my lyrics were if I didn't sound like I believed in what I recorded. This is why an efficient producer or engineer is much more than just a button pusher. It is their role to clear up the static that often occurs when an artist is attempting to communicate a message to their audience.

John opened my eyes to how the inflections and tones I chose for my beats could contradict the message of the lyrics and melody of my music. He coached me line by line through my verses, pushing me to bring out more conviction and authenticity in my voice and in every recording. He taught me how to stay in key when I sang. In the process, John gave me my first formal introduction to what it really means to produce a song and an artist.

In return, I shared with John my expertise in drum layering and mixing. I gave him a sense of the importance of spacing his instruments during the mix so that every sound gets its opportunity to shine without overpowering, or being overpowered by, the other sounds. What I lacked in music theory I made up for in musical instinct and an ear for beats.

We were used to creating alone. But when we worked together we became each other's go-to producer.

There may be an abundance of beat makers in this world, but producers are a rarity. Beat makers are like assembly lines at a factory. A beat maker's only job is to robotically produce the basic ingredients of the product. In the music industry, you don't find many beat makers getting invited to the studios because their physical presence isn't a necessity. Beat makers aren't involved in the recording process because they're simply employed to get the creative juices flowing. A music producer, on the other hand, is involved in almost every aspect of a studio session. Music producers are much more involved in the creation of a song. A music producer assists the artist in the format, composition, tone, and direction of the song. Producers help the artist make important decisions that eventually lead them into making an even better song.

> *Producers help the artist make important decisions that eventually lead them into making an even better song.*

John was a true *producer*. Collaborating with someone as musically inclined as him was a real blessing for me. Simply mirroring what he did helped me break out of my *video-gamey* shackles once and for all. And any time I had questions about chords and scales he was always willing to share his answers.

Producers, I highly suggest you find a John in your life to collaborate with early on in your career. Not just someone willing to work with you, but someone from whom you can learn as well. Someone excited to work with you and share their knowledge. Find someone looking to grow with you, someone who has strengths in areas where you want to improve.

But also make sure you're bringing something valuable to the table. In my relationship with John, my ear and experience allowed for iron to sharpen iron. We helped each other. I don't think it was a coincidence that we reconnected. I also don't think it was a coincidence that our individual weaknesses were the other's strengths.

> *Find someone to collaborate with early on in your career, someone you can teach and learn from—someone looking to grow with you.*

YOUR GREATEST INVESTMENT IS IN YOURSELF

I've had the opportunity to collaborate with several types of Hip Hop producers over the years. I've dealt with controlling producers, territorial producers, OCD producers, energetic producers, cocky producers, sloppy producers, insecure producers, we-can-do-it! producers, lazy producers, and-can-we-please-take-another-break? producers.

All this allows me to draw a few conclusions. The most important one as far as I'm concerned is this: not every producer is meant to work with another. Sometimes two people's ways of working, or their personalities, are so incongruous that you just can't get them to blend together in support of the music.

Collaboration should never be forced. If it is, the art will suffer. If it's meant to be then it will be.

Most producers I know do better work on their own anyway. To this day I still experience my most creative and enjoyable moments working alone in a studio. What's more, given the abundance of information available on the Internet today, producers don't have to go the traditional route to achieve greatness. For example, face-to-face collaborations are no longer necessary to become a Prosperous Producer (though they can still be great learning experiences).

> *So many of us have been programed by our parents, siblings, and friends, or by poverty and fear of failure, to believe that money is a more complex topic than it really is.*

Once upon a time young producers could complain about there not being enough reliable educational resources out there. When I first started to collaborate with other producers I did so because there weren't nearly as many books, YouTube tutorials, and online courses as there are today.

Today that excuse is obsolete. Just run a quick Google search and you'll find producers offering real value to their audiences. Producers like Game (BusyWorksBeats.com), Epik (EpikBeats.com), Superstar O (SuperstarO.com), OSYM (Osymbeats.com)—and me, of course, at CurtissKingBeats.com—all provide you more than just beats. It's become the norm for the leaders in our industry to offer everything from music theory courses to drum kits to producer mentorship programs.

Young producers, be thankful that you're living in a time when information is so abundant. Nowadays the bigger question is this: how much are *you* willing to invest in *yourself*?

This brings up the topic of money, which is a big one. So let's talk about it.

So many of us have been programed by our parents, siblings, and friends, or by poverty and fear of failure, to believe that money is a more complex topic than it really is. It's easy for lack of money to seem like another obstacle standing in the way of our dreams.

> ## *Money is just the echo of the value we provide.*

Before I began leasing my beats I read a book called *Rich Dad, Poor Dad* by Robert Kiyosaki. By the time I reached the final page it felt like my brain had been completely rewired to look at money for what it really is: pieces of paper. Money is just green pieces of paper that we allow to dictate our every move, our every decision—and most of all our biggest fears. The moment we stop our love affair with the idea of what money can do for us and replace it with the viewpoint that money is merely the byproduct of *how we are compensated for our value*, the quicker our relationship with money changes.

For most of my life I was taught that money is the root of all evil. That's what I believed until I heard Professor Morgan say something along these lines:

"Money isn't the root of all evil. Money is paper. Money is without emotion. Money is the magnifying-glass view into the people we truly are."

His argument was simple: we give money way too much credit. We let those green slips of paper control our lives when we should be more focused on growing ourselves and sharing our value first.

Money is just the echo of the value we provide.

Sometimes a producer will inquire about my consultation service and ask me if it's really worth my fee. They're so afraid of losing money that they try to talk themselves out of it before we even begin.

I tell them I can't answer that question for them. The question they should ask themselves, I say, is this: "Do you believe you're worth the investment?" Another question I might ask is: "Can it really be considered a financial loss when you're spending it on your potential growth and future? If you lose green pieces of paper pursuing your dreams, does it mean that your dreams are no longer worth pursuing?"

Of course not.

My message to my fellow producers is very simple: Don't be afraid to invest in yourselves.

Yes, sometimes you might be out some time or money. You can't expect to win big in life without sometimes losing big—it comes with the territory. But in the beat-leasing/producing business—and probably *any* business—acknowledging your fears without letting them interfere with what you know you must do to be successful *will allow you to become massively successful.*

> **Keep investing in the stock that promises to yield the biggest return: yourself.**

At the same time, it doesn't have to be an all-or-nothing thing. My own fearlessness when it came to investing in myself was a slow process. It started with me investing a few dollars here and there (that was all I had anyway). Once I saw even the slightest, most microscopic sign of growth I proceeded to spend a little bit more. I began to see that the more I invested in myself the more valuable I became.

Prosperous Hip Hop producers don't make excuses. We take accountability and stay creative with our solutions. Prosperous Producers strive to achieve a mindset that is rooted in abundance, not scarcity.

Keep investing in the stock that promises to yield the biggest return: yourself.

<u>Lessons to Take Away from Chapter 5</u>

1. Producers are naturally weird. Embrace your nature.
2. Perfect the equipment you have and make upgrades when necessary.
3. Become a better producer faster through mirroring and collaborating.
4. Money is the echo of the value we provide.
5. Don't be afraid to invest in yourself!

CHAPTER 6

THE SAMPLE

"Don't build your empire strictly off of sampling."

~ Murs

The art of sampling is as old as Hip Hop itself. The act of repurposing sounds from other sounds to tell a story may even be as old as music itself.

Sampling is the backbone of music production in Hip Hop. The dictionary describes sampling as "the technique of digitally encoding music or sound and reusing it as part of a composition or recording."[6] Sampling for me has always been the equivalent of reconnecting with an old friend and helping them tell their story in a contemporary fashion. Much of the success that I enjoy today has been built on the foundation of sampling.

---

[6] "Sampling | Definition of sampling in US English by Oxford Dictionaries." Oxford Dictionaries | English. Accessed December 11, 2017. https://en.oxforddictionaries.com/definition/us/sampling.

A SAMPLE OF MY LIFE

Something I like to do from time to time is meet up with my good friends Billie Holiday and Nina Simone for a drink at the local coffee shop. If they happen to be busy I hit up my other buddy, Bob Marley, to see if he wants to go to the park and shoot some hoops. On the weekends when Bob is busy, you might catch me at a local jazz café checking out a set by my Rat Pack friends Frank Sinatra, Dean Martin, and Sammy Davis Jr. Unfortunately, because their shows run so late I have to leave before their last song so I don't oversleep and miss my early morning orchestra lessons with Quincy Jones and Barry White.

As you can tell, my life is often a chaotic musical masterpiece.

> *Sampling is the backbone of Hip Hop. It gives producers like me and you the opportunity to work with and reimagine the classic works of legends.*

The art of sampling makes these imaginary scenarios an everyday reality in my head. No matter what direction Hip Hop goes musically, the sampling always seems to follow close behind. Once again I must state, sampling is the backbone of Hip Hop. It gives producers like me and you the opportunity to work with and reimagine the classic works of legends who died before we were born.

When I think about my favorite Hip Hop songs growing up, it's not an exaggeration to say that at least 85 to 90 percent of them included samples. Back then a lot of my elders talked down about Hip Hop's use of samples (maybe they still do). They'd complain about how rappers and producers were stealing a good thing and ruining it. I understood why they felt like that about the repurposing of their beloved records—but I always disagreed with them. For me, sampling was the gateway drug to my addiction to the sounds of the past.

Growing up with divorced parents often made me feel pretty damn lucky. I got two birthday celebrations, two Christmases, and best of all: two completely different tastes in music. My dad listened to funk bands like Cameo, Con Funk Shun and Earth, Wind & Fire. My mom listened to singers like Lionel Richie and Marvin Gaye, and to bands like the Doobie Brothers. In other words, I was lucky enough to grow up in two different households that each shared a deep appreciation of good music.

I've always felt like an old man in a young body, and part of the reason for that may be my parents and their broad musical preferences. Unlike other kids my age I loved the music my parents and grandparents used to play. I'd pick my grandfather Charles's brain and ask him why he loved the music he did. The smile he wore while listening to his favorite Curtis Mayfield records made me curious about where they took him mentally. And since my grandfather was a great storyteller, he loved to tell me stuff like where he was at the first time he heard certain songs, who he was with, what he was feeling and so on. Listening to him talk about his favorite songs was like watching a photo album in motion.

GRANDPA'S VINYL COLLECTION

In the early 1990s my grandfather Charles had an extensive collection of 8-track tapes, cassette tapes, and vinyl records of all shapes and sizes. Way before the thought of becoming a music producer even crossed my mind, I spent hours and hours going through his music collection. The only thing I wasn't allowed to do at that age was try to play those easily scratched records without asking an adult first.

Some of the artwork on those record covers was hilarious. All that funk and Motown vinyl was plastered with images of men from the 1970s wearing fur coats, bell bottoms, and silk shirts that conveniently showed off their wild chest hair. I used to joke with my grandfather that their chest hair reminded me of freshly cooked taco meat. Other times I'd come across vinyls with beautiful black women sporting big afros—and nothing else. My favorite vinyl covers were the colorfully animated ones that my mom had contributed to his collection. Because those covers drew me in first, I found myself at a very young age falling in love with the music of the legendary Bootsy Collins.

When I was finally old enough to play my grandfather's records without adult supervision, a whole new world opened up to me. Growing up I'd been taught never to judge a book by its cover. And throughout my extensive crate digging I applied that principle by never judging a vinyl by the taco-meat chest hair of the guys on its cover.

There was no feeling in the world quite like listening to that soulful music on its original vinyl using a vintage record player. The music felt warmer and more pristine, more organic and alive. I witnessed music's ability to change the temperature of a room. Having this warmer connection with music was insanely important to me—it's why my relationship with the music I create today is so raw.

Sometimes my mom would come in and enjoy whatever music I was playing. During these impromptu listening sessions she'd teach me how to play a game that tested how well I was listening. Every time I started a new record I had to try my best to name all the instruments being played in the song in under a minute. Without even realizing it, this game was going to one day help make me an amazing producer.

CAN YOU TEACH ME HOW TO SAMPLE?

I have been blessed to have some great friends. Victor Martinez is one of them. I met Vic in 2002 at Downey High School. He came into my life at the perfect time, when I was searching deep within myself for the answers to who I was. He reminded me of something my father once taught me: a man can't know who he is unless he first understands where he and his ancestors came from. Vic identified himself as Chicano. He'd often explain to me how important his Brown Pride was in his pursuit to find out who he was. He encouraged me as a black man to pursue the same knowledge and pride in my culture. (Then right when our conversations were getting too serious he'd break it up by joking about how much I talked like Braxton from *The Jamie Foxx Show*.)

There was one thing we did more than talk about the need to uplift our people: we clowned the living hell out of each other. He believed that it helped us create thicker skins. He was right.

There have been so many disrespectful things said about me in this industry over the years. The only reason I could take them on the chin and smile is because they didn't even scratch the surface of the disrespect Vic and I used to sling at one another for fun. We were like comedian Dave Chappelle in the "Player Haters Ball" skit; we turned hate into comedy to build and strengthen each other's characters.

Vic and I also connected because of our love of Hip Hop. We were both aspiring emcees, even if his lyrics were light years ahead of mine. His were more clever, detailed and honest than mine, which were pretty good because of my work with Keyden. But listening to Vic's made me feel like my own needed a lot more work to improve.

In 2002, Blacks and Mexicans didn't have the best relationship in Southern California. Fights and rumors of a race war were brewing every other week at my high school. When Vic and I hung out together, it caused a lot of confusion for some people. But we didn't care. In fact, we often spoke about doing whatever we could to help ease the tensions between our people at school.

One day we came up with an idea to collaborate on a song called "Stereotypes." We ended up loving it so much that we played it for some of the school officials. They liked it too—so much so that they allowed us to perform it at our school's culture day event. It was the first show ever for both of us.

We graduated in 2003, but years later Vic was one of the few people I still kept in constant contact with. As a producer, you need people around who will tell you the truth no matter how ugly it might be. Vic was one of those trusted people for me. I'd play him the new collaborations John and I were working on and he wouldn't hold any punches with his critiques. At the end of the day, some of the music he liked and some of it just wasn't for him.

Vic's critiques taught me a valuable lesson that I think is worth sharing. Producers, it is important to keep in mind that every critique you receive, good or bad, is the opinion of another human being. Everyone has their own idea of how amazing music should sound. While it's important for your growth that you respect these opinions, it is just as important that you first qualify these suggestions. Whenever you receive critiques, first question the source of the critique. Ask yourself if this person's taste in music aligns with your taste, and I guarantee it will help you decide whether or not you want to take their advice.

> *As a producer, you need people around who will tell you the truth no matter how ugly it might be.*

YOU DID THAT ON FRUITYLOOPS?

As I started transitioning from making beats on my PlayStation to adopting John's live recording process, Vic began learning to make beats on a program called FruityLoops (or FL Studio). In the early 2000s FruityLoops had a bad reputation among older, hardware-based producers. To them a producer using FruityLoops was a joke and not serious about his or her career. In their eyes, FruityLoops was a cheap way to get into the production game.

Like an idiot, I listened to them.

I slowly progressed at making beats John's way, and Vic kept getting better with FruityLoops. He loved sampling the classic oldies that he grew up on, breathing new life into classic songs like "Two Lovers" by Mary Wells or "La-La Means I Love You" by the Delfonics. He'd chop each sample up with the precision of a heart surgeon. Sometimes he'd rearrange samples so well that songs I grew up listening to became unrecognizable. For a sample-based Hip Hop producer that's the ultimate challenge and compliment.

I, on the other hand, sucked terribly at sampling. When I tried to emulate the sampling techniques of my favorite producers the result was often awkward and out of sync. It didn't help that sampling was a skill that required cohesive synching, basic math, and knowing what to sample. In the beginning I wanted to sample *everything*—and I hated math.

Regardless, I committed to becoming a better sampling producer after watching Vic work. I desperately wanted to revisit some of the beautiful records I used to listen to in my grandpa's collection. I wanted to stop wandering aimlessly through a sampler's abyss and just ask Vic if he could show me the way.

When I finally did, he didn't hesitate to help. But he warned me that I'd also have to get a crash course in FruityLoops in order to fully understand his process. Going against my own (uninformed) reservations about the program, I agreed to learn all about it.

In less than two hours Vic broke down each part of his sampling process on FruityLoops as follows:

- Find a sample with minimal drums and words
- If the sample does have words, look for the parts with soft choir "Ooos" and "Ahhs"
- If your sample has drums, make sure their time signature is 4/4 and not 3/4

- Open the sample up in Edison (an editing tool)
- Highlight, loop, and grab anything you hear that sounds special
- List all your samples on your FruityLoops sequencer
- Open the FruityLoops Slicer tool
- Determine if you want the sample to be slower or faster
- Find the pitch you want the sample to be adjusted to
- Find the tempo using the metronome
- Lay your snare down first to match the timing of the sample
- Start chopping, mixing, and matching the sample clips until the puzzle is complete

> *By matching his drums to the natural rhythms of the oldies bands that he was sampling, his drums sounded just as natural as their live drummers.*

There was something about the way Vic explained the process of sampling that completely demystified the process. The ease of his beat-making process also made me look at FruityLoops from a whole new perspective. Vic's beats didn't sound robotic or cheap, like the older producers said FruityLoops beats sounded. Because of Vic's sampling skills, he didn't have to worry about learning swing the way I did. By matching his drums to the natural rhythms of the oldies bands that he was sampling, his drums sounded just as natural as their live drummers. I remember looking at him after he played certain beats and asking him, "Did you really do that all on FruityLoops?"

MAKING THE CHANGE TO FRUITYLOOPS

So just when I'd begun to fall in love with the new beat-making process that John had taught me, FruityLoops came along and crashed the party. Before my session with Vic that night, John and I chose to believe all the bad things hardware producers had said about FruityLoops. We made fun of it without ever giving it a chance. Even after I told John about my new outlook on FruityLoops, he was still convinced that his process was the best for him. He didn't really have much interest in converting to the gospel of FruityLoops. But after I had that very first session with Vic I became a dedicated believer. As far as I could see, the FruityLoops approach would be the future of music production.

Vic graciously hooked me up with a copy of FruityLoops and I wasted no time installing it on my computer that night. When I first started snooping around the program, trying carefully to remember all the things Vic had taught me, I was surprised by how familiar it all looked—there were so many similarities between the layouts of FruityLoops and my old friend *MTV Music Generator,* including layout colors, pattern blocks, library

> **Once I saw the value of FruityLoops I decided never to let others in my industry tell me what I could or couldn't use to create my music.**

titles, and overall user friendliness. I immediately felt at home with the new program; it reminded me of the feeling I had when I first started making beats. And as I worked with it day by day I started to feel like I'd been preparing for FruityLoops my whole career. The only difference was that this time I had a better idea of what I was doing.

When I chose to move to FruityLoops I made a commitment to myself that I was going to learn that damn program no matter how difficult it got. I finished my first beat in less than an hour. FruityLoops allowed me to get my ideas out faster than ever before. I kept working at it in the days and weeks that followed, discovering all the features FL Studio provided. If I didn't know what a button did,

I'd press it and learn the hard way.

I was proud of myself for adapting and taking a chance, for being flexible enough to overcome my initial prejudice against the program. It felt like I was becoming more open-minded and advancing with the times. For me, using FruityLoops was more than just a subtle shift in beat programs. My switch signaled a decision to go fearlessly against the traditional producer grain. Thank God it ended up working out for me. And it wasn't the last time I did something like that. In fact, once I saw the value of FruityLoops I decided never to let others in my industry tell me what I could or couldn't use to create *my* music.

Almost fourteen years later I still use FL Studio to create music. Programs such as FL Studio, Reason, Ableton, and Logic lead the way today in advancing the technology of music production. I am thankful to these companies for providing such brilliant products that allow both young and old producers to find a common ground in our pursuit of creating the best music possible—even if we happen to be doing it from the comfort of our bedrooms.

Lessons to Take Away from Chapter 6

1. Learning the art of sampling will make you a better producer.
2. Sometimes life prepares us early on for our future.
3. Listen to as much different music as you can; the broader your listening range the more ideas you have to draw on.
4. Be flexible and open to change.
5. Don't allow the industry or old ways of thinking to dictate your musical direction.

CHAPTER 7

THE **MELODY**

"We are the music-makers,
And we are the dreamers of dreams . . ."

~ Willy Wonka[7]

W hen I was younger, I would help my grandmother make her homemade lemon cake from scratch. She showed me a trick her own mother had taught her to make her cakes extra lemony on the inside. Before she applied the glaze she would use a toothpick to poke around the cake so that the syrup could travel directly to the center. This way every slice of the cake was sure to be just as lemony as the first.

In many ways I have approached the melody in my beat as the

---

7 Originally from "Ode," a poem by Arthur William Edgar O'Shaughnessy, published in Music and Moonlight (1874).

glaze that sweetens the overall production. Since I began making beats I have always started with the drums, just as a baker starts with the eggs, butter, and cake flour. As soon as I finished cooking up the drums, the melody represented that sweet lemony glaze that I could apply to the outer layer and which would then infuse the whole song. Fittingly, without any traditional music training I found myself doing a lot of poking around on my keyboard in order to find the perfect melodic sweet spot.

ENTRY-LEVEL MARKETING CERTIFICATE

> *Marketing is the vehicle we use to clearly communicate the value of a product to an audience. An effective marketing campaign can take a customer on a journey just like a good beat can.*

When I first chose to attend Orange Coast College in 2005 I had intentions of doing what probably every other aspiring producer on campus was there to do: join the music production program and earn my certificate. But by my second semester I was falling madly in love with the world of marketing, thanks to Professor Morgan. His teaching style was simplifying a field I'd always seen as extremely complex and confusing. He made me look at marketing in much the same way that I looked at making a beat.

When as producers we make a beat, our goal is to convey a clear message. We make beats with specific elements meant to take the listener on a journey. Through music we have the ability to make our listener feel sad, happy, excited, angry and more. Every instrument we choose communicates another piece of emotion.

Marketing is the vehicle we use to clearly communicate the value of a product to an audience. An effective marketing campaign can take a customer on a journey just like a good beat can. Both require creating something that resonates with the listener and makes them feel something.

This epiphany came to me in Professor Morgan's "Principles of Advertising" class while I was working on a group project with my classmates. The project required us to come up with an ad campaign to save a fictional zoo that was struggling with sales. We had to formulate a comprehensive rebranding of the zoo using hip, modern advertisements. The group put me in charge of creating a one-minute radio jingle for the zoo campaign.

This was the first time I'd ever been in charge of creating a piece of music that wasn't Hip Hop-related. The project both excited and scared the hell out of me. I didn't know the first thing about making music kids would like. I sat with FruityLoops and my piano for hours as I tooth-picked at every piano key, trying to find something special. After about three hours I came up with a melody and phrase I was happy with. The song's lyrics were simply:

"I want to go to the zooooo today!"

As silly as it might sound, creating my first jingle was one of my proudest musical moments. I ended up hiring my baby sister Paige to sing the words—for the expensive price of a bag of Skittles. (She was obviously a tough negotiator.) About thirty minutes and twelve takes later she nailed the jingle. In post-production I added zoo animal sound effects and a soft conga drum loop. I even added in myself as a narrator; I spoke directly to parents about all the great deals the zoo had to offer. Before I knew it, the jingle was complete.

The next day my group had to present our ad campaign, which meant I had to play my commercial in front of the whole class. To be honest, I felt a bit silly sharing something so "childish" sounding with a classroom full of aspiring businessmen and women. But they loved it. Even Professor Morgan, who isn't known for giving over-the-top praise, nodded his head in approval. No words can describe the joy that moment brought me as I walked back to my desk, hi-fiving with my group along the way.[8]

As class let out for the night, Professor Morgan asked if I could stay for a few minutes to discuss something important. He was curious about what my plans were at OCC and whether I'd heard about his entry-level marketing certificate program. I shared my music production aspirations with him and said I hadn't heard of his program— but was all ears.

Scan the QR code to hear the zoo jingle.

He said, "If you finish this course and my other two marketing courses you'll walk out of here with an entry-level marketing certificate. I wanted to tell you about this because you showed great potential with that jingle you presented today."

One thing about me: it doesn't take much to fill me up with motivation, especially if I look up to you. I certainly looked up to Professor Morgan because of the way he handled himself and how he discussed the art of business. And as I've already said, the way he taught marketing reminded me of how I make beats. We were both passionate about our fields and about helping others achieve their highest levels of success. And the fact that he was so far removed from my own field of beat-making made his compliment about my marketing potential feel even more special.

I'd already been excited about his class, but hearing about the

---

[8] Zoo jingle:
https://www.youtube.com/watch?v=oW323bpHZpY&list=WL&index=20

certificate program was icing on the cake. Before I left for the night he provided me a few papers with additional information about the entry-level marketing certificate program.

It was starting to look like I was going to leave this campus with a piece of paper indicating my completion of a program.

MYSPACE LAYOUTS FOR SALE

Creating that zoo jingle gave me a new definition of what it meant to think outside the box. It made me believe I was capable of doing so much more than just making beats. It also made me question why more people in my field weren't banging down my door looking to work with me. I knew how to do a lot, but for some reason I was only working with my close friends. So I asked myself: how can I become more valuable to my peers?

Then I was reminded of something Professor Morgan said. "If you want to be a part of the elite in your industry, provide a service they all need. You will increase your worth to your network."

> *I asked myself:* **How can I become more valuable to my peers?**

Those words resonated with me deeply, because in an industry that was all about doing for *self*, this line of thinking was a contradiction. But, ironically, that's why I liked it. This type of thinking inspired me to go against the grain. So, when I made the decision to pursue my entry-level marketing certificate, I also committed myself to learning a few skills that could make me more valuable to my industry.

The next few months I taught myself how to do graphic design on Adobe Photoshop, vocal mixing on Adobe Audition, and video editing on Windows Movie Maker. I knew that if I could somehow become above-average in at least one of these areas I would have rappers knocking at my door. It wouldn't matter if they didn't like my beats—they would at least need my graphic design skills for their album covers, my html knowledge for their Myspace pages, or my video-editing skills for their music videos.

The more I learned the better I became in every area I focused on. I started combining everything I taught myself about graphic design with what I'd been learning in my "Principles of Advertising" class and putting it to work on my Myspace page. I used to spend hours perfecting the layouts of my Myspace page. In fact, I became so good at it that I became one of the first Myspace musicians to utilize moving gifs as an advertising tool to attract new friend requests. I designed a new Myspace layout for myself every time I dropped a new song or beat. I spent many hours combing through YouTube videos searching for new graphic design and video-editing tutorials. I probably would've spent even more hours researching if I didn't have to go to work at my sandwich job each morning.

To say I was getting sick of that job would be a tragic understatement. Between school and my own self-education—both of which were giving me an unbelievable high—the only thing that could consistently bring me down was my job. My mentality was still about taking the good with the bad, but things were really starting to get out of hand. I told myself that if I could just make an extra $100-$300 a month I could combine that with my financial aid checks and quit my sandwich job for good.

At this stage of my production career I wasn't even thinking about the possibility of selling my beats. This was still many years before I met any of my beat-selling mentors. What stopped me from trying was my self-limiting belief that my beats were too weird to rap on for most rappers who weren't my friends. My homies used to encourage me to sell my beats but I felt like I still had too much growing to do. I occasionally thought about charging *them*, but I was too embarrassed to ask my friends to pay me for my beats. They were, after all, the same friends who had encouraged and pushed me to keep going early on.

As I continued to drop new songs and designs on my Myspace page, I found myself receiving compliments from strangers on my design work. Initially it didn't click in my mind that this was a service I could charge for. But one day at work I came up with an idea to offer my Myspace design work as a paid service for rappers and producers.

I counted down the hours until I could finally leave the sandwich shop that day, getting more and more excited at the prospect. I got home around 11:00 p.m. and stayed up until about 7:00 a.m. designing a new Myspace page for my design service. When I finally finished, I went to sleep for a couple of hours, only to start working at it again when I woke up. When I was all set to go, I began adding random rapper and producer profiles, hoping to attract potential customers. When a musician profile added me as a friend I sent a generic comment to their page that read:

Thanks for the add! If you ever need a custom Myspace layout hit me up!

About two weeks passed and not one person hit me back.

I was discouraged but not defeated. My disgust for my job far outweighed the disappointment of not immediately getting any customers. Then one day, out of the blue, a rapper from Arizona hit me up in my inbox. He told me he was very impressed with my graphic design work and wanted to know about my rates. I responded immediately, informing him that I charged $50 for a custom Myspace layout. I also added that customers paid $25 to get started and another $25 upon completion of their layout. I assured him that most orders were delivered within forty-eight hours. In short, I tried everything in the book to assure him that I provided great customer service.

An hour ticked past without a sound.

I started questioning myself. *Was $50 too much to ask? This is my* *first potential customer—should I give him a break?*

I asked myself about twenty more self-doubting questions and then decided to review some of my notes from my Professional Selling class with Professor Morgan:

Professor Morgan: *Your price is your price; stand by it confidently!*

I read that quote a few times and chose to patiently await a reply. About twenty minutes later he responded.

AZ Rapper: Ok, cool. I'll send that first $25 now. What's your PayPal info?

Wait, what?!

I couldn't believe it was that easy. I started jumping around my patio, fist-pumping like a kid who's rolled a bumper-assisted strike at the bowling alley. I thought, *This is about to be your first rap money!*

After his first payment was processed I began asking him questions about what he was looking for in his Myspace design.

The AZ rapper explained he wanted a design that represented Arizona, like a scene out of an old western. He wanted me to incorporate a bunch of things like tumbleweeds, spurs, and old barn doors. As I read his description I immediately got a vision of exactly how I wanted to approach the design. About seven hours later I completed the layout. I sent him a watermarked preview of it and went to bed.

> **"Your price is your price; stand by it confidently!"**
>
> **~ Professor Morgan**

The next morning his reaction was waiting for me in my inbox.

AZ Rapper: WOOOOOOOOOOOOOOOOWWWW!!!!!!!!!! You killed this design! I'm sending over the other $25 now!

I checked my email after reading the message. Sure enough, he had sent the other $25. I had officially made my first piece of rap-related money. I was so excited about my first customer that I was physically prepared that day to quit my job. I say "physically" because mentally I knew damn well I couldn't survive on $50 with a pending $375 Volkswagen Passat car note.

It was a good thing I didn't quit. Little did I know that not only would this be my first Myspace layout sell, but also my last. For the next month my Myspace layout business was completely dry, so I decided to hang it up. BUT, this was an unbelievable moment, and a huge step in the right direction. For the first time I realized I actually *could* make money with my growing skillset.

Next semester at OCC I took the two classes required to complete the marketing certificate program: "Introduction to Marketing" and "Professional Selling." I could have signed up for music production classes but instead went against the grain again and signed up for acting and singing classes.

That semester was the most fun I'd ever had at school. To me, that was what school was supposed to feel like. I was learning skills that, if practiced and put into action, could make me not only a better businessman and artist but a better human being. I woke up every day looking forward to going to school.

GOODBYE OCC

I completed my classes with high marks. On the last day of our "Introduction to Marketing" class Professor Morgan handed out our Entry-Level Marketing certificates. Most of my classmates saw these as just minor checkpoints on the way to their associate degrees. But for me, this *was* my degree. If you could've seen me when Professor Morgan called my name that night you would've sworn I was walking down the classroom aisle with a cap and gown on. I was smiling from ear to ear because I was so proud of myself. Driving home I played "I Wonder" by Kanye West at deafening levels and cried like a baby.

Why was this such a powerful experience for me?

OCC was a getaway on many levels. But now, with this certificate in hand, it signaled the end of an era. It was the end of my collegiate oasis. It was back home to Carson for me, where I was surrounded by an environment that most of my classmates never experienced. They never had to worry what colors they were allowed to wear day-to-day. They didn't have to have ridiculous mental debates about whether it was worth the risk to get gas at certain hours of the night. But I did, and that was home for me. My honeymoon with OCC was officially over.

It was time to take the next steps.

Lessons to Take Away from Chapter 7

1. Set goals and keep them close till you accomplish them.
2. Sometimes your best musical breakthroughs come outside of your comfort zone.
3. Never hesitate to learn new skills that will potentially make you more valuable to your industry, even if those skills at first don't seem directly connected to your industry.
4. Making rap money is an amazing feeling. Create avenues to make it possible.

CHAPTER 8

THE BASS

"The bassline is the direct vibration of the soul."

~ Yep (Tomorrow, Yesterday)

When I first started making beats I underestimated the importance of the bassline. My first ten beats didn't have a single instrument in the sub frequency. I wasn't like most of my testosterone-driven peers who were addicted to the low end, but maybe this was why my peers didn't initially feel my beats. As my friend Yep brilliantly points out above, the bass is the direct vibration of the soul. No wonder my peers felt disconnected.

The more experienced I became as a producer, the more I realized what the bassline means to a beat: the warmth of wholeness. It warms and amplifies the drums and melody. Symbolically, the bassline was the head nod Professor Morgan gave for my zoo jingle. It was the feeling of my first placement. I'm sure you've had—and will keep having—your own bassline moments; you know them when you feel them.

WELCOME TO CARSON, CALIFORNIA

Having that certificate of completion gave me an insatiable appetite for success. I'd never experienced anything like it before. I wanted more as a producer—more growth, more equipment upgrades, and most of all more collaborations with rappers. In 2008, the only artists who rapped over my beats were my friends and myself. I was grateful for the music we created but I wanted to experience another level of artistry. I wanted to branch out.

I realized that if this was a goal I truly desired it would make sense to search around my neighborhood for artists to work with. But I lived in Carson, California, not Andy Griffith's Mayberry. I'd gone to elementary and middle school in Carson and I knew the city very well. Carson can be very misleading when you first visit it. You may see the multitude of beautiful two-story homes with well-kept lawns and luxury cars in the driveways and assume it to be like every other affluent, safe, suburban African-American neighborhood in America. But those of us living in Carson during the late 1990s saw things much differently.

Carson is located dead smack in the middle of Compton and Long Beach. Before the addition of the StubHub Center stadium, you didn't hear much about Carson in the mainstream news cycle unless it was something about a violent crime. Looks were so misleading that as a fourteen-year-old child I didn't realize how dangerous it could be. But I found out one day in middle school when I decided to wear a new pair of red and white Jordans to school.

As I walked around that day I kept noticing my classmates giving me dirty looks and shaking their heads. I assumed it was because I had the newest Jordans and they didn't. Little did I know my classmates were looking at me like I was a dead man walking.

A friend stopped me during lunch and said, "Dawg, why did you wear those? You better run home after school before them 190s see you with those on. They might try to KILL YOU, dawg!"

190s? Kill Me?

Unbeknownst to me, the 190s were a local Crip gang in Carson, and they were represented by the color blue. For those of you who don't know, the red in my Jordans was symbolic of their rival gang, the Bloods. Chills rushed down my spine when my friend gave me this news. For the first time ever I experienced what it felt like to be a human target. But there was nothing I could do about it unless I chose to walk around school barefoot. I just had to deal until I got picked up at the end of the day.

When school let out I stood outside scanning the street for my dad's car. I said about twenty silent prayers as I caught cold stares from older kids with tattoos . . . and *blue* shoes. Mind you, this was years before everyone had a smartphone, so I couldn't call my dad to check his ETA. I just had to sit there and hope nobody pressed me about my shoes.

> **Carson was not a city to be tested, but it made me stronger and it will always be a part of who I am.**

When my dad's Camry finally pulled up I sprinted over to it immediately. But before I reached the passenger door somebody said, in a calm yet authoritative voice:

OG Crip: "C careful out here, lil cuh, with them shoes on."

I nodded my head and vowed never to wear those shoes to school again.

That occasion and many others like it left a bad taste in my mouth when I thought of my lovely city. Carson was not a city to be tested.

Even though it was nowhere near as bad as neighboring Compton, sometimes it was just bad enough that even a square like me had to be aware of his surroundings.

But don't get me wrong: I LOVED Carson for all the positive it did for my self-esteem and for all the friends I made there. The city made me stronger and helped me develop a level of street smarts I'm thankful to have. I was proud to call it home, and it will always be a part of who I am.

In fact, my stage name, "Curtiss King," was partly derived from the middle school I attended: Curtiss Middle School.

WE SHOULD CALL OURSELVES "CURTISS KING"

In the blazing Carson summer heat of 2004, John and I spent a ton of time on my humid patio developing an amazing chemistry as collaborative producers. My sessions with John were vital to my growth as a producer. Watching him play the keys and being able to interrupt him to ask question after question was an incredible opportunity. For example, I'd ask him why certain chords felt different from others, and he'd answer me in great detail.

I was also getting very comfortable with FruityLoops and still getting sampling lessons with Victor on the weekends. (Around this time, FruityLoops made some transitions of their own and rebranded themselves as FL Studio.) Between John and Victor I felt myself becoming a more well-rounded producer.

Around 2005 John and I came up with the idea of giving our production duo a name. Since we had met at Curtiss Middle School and he went to high school at King/Drew Magnet High School of Medicine and Science in Los Angeles, we decided to call our duo CURTISS KING.

Yes, Curtiss King started off as a production duo and not one person.

Another one of my childhood friends, Chris McMullen, just so happened to be one of our biggest supporters. Chris was thoroughly impressed with the music his former classmates were creating together. He would brag to his Morehouse College homies about how amazing our collaborations were turning out. He also had a younger brother named Josh who was starting to rap. One day, Chris decided to bring Josh to my studio so he could see what Curtiss King Productions was creating.

Josh's rap name was $J.O.$. After hearing him rap, John and I thought it would be dope to produce some original beats for him. So J.O. was one of the first artists I produced. He allowed me not just to make the beats for him, but also to give him suggestions on how to improve his recording techniques. For him, making music on my patio represented an escape from the kind of lifestyle that I'd run away from years ago in a pair of white-and-red Jordans.

J.O. did a great job making me forget that that part of life still existed. We spent most of our sessions recording, laughing, and talking about life. He was just as funny as he was intelligent. He was young but talented beyond his years, and he brought a fresh, youthful vibe to the studio.

As John and I worked on music for ourselves and J.O., we started getting hungry to do it more and more. John came up with the idea of bringing J.O. under our umbrella and turning Curtiss King Productions into a record label. I loved the idea and thought it would be a great opportunity to network with new artists and sharpen our skills as musicians.

GETTING OUT

John and I spent a lot of time together in the studio, but he was the only one of us who still had a social life. I was a studio rat, a hermit, so driven to become a better producer that I'd stopped going out entirely. Thankfully my growth as a producer wasn't predicated on me leaving the house.

John felt differently. Going out and being around people gave his life much needed balance and new energy. He even felt it improved his workflow when he returned to the studio.

Our friend Chris felt the same way. So one night I reluctantly pried my fingers away from my MIDI controller and allowed John and Chris to get me out of the house. We went to visit some of their old high school friends at their UCLA dorms.

> *I went out more often and slowly started coming out of my shell. All the energy sparked new, creative ideas in me and gave me a look inside the mind of the average music consumer.*

Surprisingly, as the night wore on I began to see how this new environment was exactly what I needed. Being around so many young, intelligent men and women who were excited about life was ideal. So I went out with Chris and John more often, and I slowly started coming out of my shell. All the energy sparked new, creative ideas in me. Listening to these students describe the kinds of music they were into and why they liked it gave me a crucial look inside the mind of the average music consumer. Additionally, listening to their honest feedback on the music John and I were creating was crucial, because it was well-articulated and genuinely constructive.

I was also forced to become more social, and this in turn made me want to be around people more often. Producers know how lonely the studio can be at times, especially in the beginning. Inspired by all of these new experiences, John and I decided to bring in four more artists under the Curtiss King Productions brand: a Christian rapper named A. Nameless, my friend Victor, an emcee from John's college named Ignacio, and a female emcee named Bella Donna.

We had a lot of work stacked up and I was excited about it. Everything was starting to come together for Curtiss King Productions. We were recording multiple albums, we had a posse cut, and John and I were becoming better producers. I even got my first tattoo: the original Curtiss King logo.

Then one night, out of the blue, John called and asked if I could meet him at his house in twenty minutes.

THE BREAKUP OF CURTISS KING PRODUCTIONS

John had been missing in action from studio sessions for a few days. I didn't know what was up, but as it turns out he'd been going through a lot of personal issues that were making him question his purpose and sense of duty to his strong religious beliefs. He asked himself how a career creating secular music was interfering with his personal and spiritual growth. These internal debates were so strong that he told me he wanted to quit our duo and take a long hiatus away from music.

Selfishly, I tried my best to talk him out of it. All I could think about was what we were building and how terrible his timing was. In hindsight I understand that as his friend and comrade I should have invested more energy into understanding why he felt the way he did—instead of trying to make him change his mind.

In any case, despite my efforts to keep us together, by the end of that conversation Curtiss King Productions was no more.

I wish I could give you a triumphant story of how I bounced back the next day with forty new beats, but that's not what happened. I was crushed. John was irreplaceable—not just as a musician but as a friend. His energy made me believe I could do anything as a *producer* regardless of my shortcomings as a *musician*. He had a knack for making otherwise difficult tasks sound simple. His decision angered and saddened me. But more than anything else it made me feel extremely overwhelmed. I had to deliver beats for six rappers, including myself, with limited resources.

The label was all on my shoulders and I wasn't ready for it to be that way. I was in way over my head.

Then one day I took hold of my thoughts and got realistic. My first order of business was to call each artist and explain that I was moving in a new direction with Curtiss King Productions after John's departure. I gave each artist the option of continuing to work with me but freed them from the umbrella of Curtiss King Productions. Most of them left; J.O. was the only artist who ended up staying.

John and I didn't speak much those following months, mostly due to my own pride and anger about how things unfolded. It wasn't until a year later that we had a brutally honest heart-to-heart at Chris's house, where we said everything we hadn't before. This allowed us to start our friendship moving in the right direction again.

If it wasn't for J.O. staying, I don't think I would've tried to produce other artists for a very long time. Working with him kept me focused, even though my beats weren't sounding as good without John's touch. I shared with J.O. my goal of working with artists of a different creative caliber and he immediately started naming local rappers I should reach out to. Without him knowing it, he became my ear on the streets when it came to local rappers who were supremely talented but off my radar.

> **The label was all on my shoulders and I wasn't ready for it. I was in way over my head.**

I researched maybe six rappers on Myspace. This was around 2006 and the Internet was changing the music industry. Nobody knew it at the time but websites like Myspace and Reverbnation were about to level the playing field for the "small guy" in the rap game. Although rappers like 50 Cent and Jay-Z had a monopoly on the mass media coverage of Hip Hop, the Internet gave us an alternative too alluring to ignore. Now we had the power to find the *next* 50 and Jay-Z recording out of a basement in Rhode Island, New York—or on a patio in Carson, CA.

At the time most local rappers were wrapped up in either the hyphy movement—driven by the Bay Area Hip Hop—or the clever lyricism of rappers like Lil Wayne. During one of my Myspace searches for local artists I found a rapper who stood out: Bin Ghrimm. He was a member of a Carson-based rap collective called Top Notch. Ghrimm had one of the deepest rap voices I'd ever heard. Lyrically he reminded me of a cross between Nas and Scarface, combined with the charismatic wit of Lil Wayne. I'd never heard a rapper like him, so I immediately reached out to see if he'd be interested in working together. He was, and we made plans to meet at my house the following week.

BIN GHRIMM, YOUNG MAGIC, AGENT J, & $J.O.$

Earlier in this chapter I painted a picture of what Carson was like in my younger years. Unfortunately, the older I became the more things remained the same. So maybe you can imagine how nervous I was about inviting strangers into my mom's house. I was bringing them into a studio containing all my equipment. I'd heard some pretty crazy stories from friends who'd had their home studios robbed shortly after inviting strangers over. But J.O. assured me everything would be cool, and he dropped by to sit in on my first session with Bin Ghrimm.

Ghrimm was such a dope human being. When he finally arrived and we started chopping it up with one another I felt like an idiot for being so paranoid. He was an intelligent college student with a big heart for his family, a passion for music, and a relentless hunger to prove that he was the best emcee alive.

A few minutes into things Ghrimm asked if it was cool if a few of his fellow comrades, Agent J and Young Magic, came through. I agreed, and minutes later they arrived on my doorstep. Our first thirty minutes consisted mostly of small talk about sports, sneakers, Hip Hop, women, and the projects everyone was currently working on.

After we'd covered all the typical rap subjects we started having some awkward silences. During one of these I asked everyone if they wanted to hear some of my beats. Everyone nodded in agreement.

Suddenly the air was circulating with energy and ideas; it's amazing how the right production can make that happen. All I heard as I played the beats were sounds of approval. Imagine my relief.

I played ten beats and then, for the eleventh, I hit on THE ONE.

This was a loud, 808-driven drum loop with dirty orchestral hits reminiscent of the slamming locker door sounds on The Clipse's classic song "Grindin'." Everyone in the room immediately started writing feverishly. I don't even remember any of us discussing a concept for the song. I started formatting the beat so I too could get to writing.

> *They were used to an environment where if a song had three verses and there were four rappers in the room, the last man writing wouldn't make the cut.*

Ghrimm, Young Magic, and Agent J finished their verses in less than twenty minutes. Before that day I'd never experienced writing so fast in the studio. But to them this was business as usual. They were used to an environment where if a song had three verses and there were four rappers in the room, the last man writing wouldn't make the cut. I, on the other hand, wrote at a rather average speed because most of the time I was just competing with myself. I tried not to allow their speed to distract me from writing, but I was sincerely blown away, and eventually everyone was waiting on me to finish. The last time I felt pressure like that was when I took my SAT test.

Now in reality this pressure was all in my mind. Nobody seemed to be particularly concerned with how long I was taking to write, but the voice in my head said they were. And ask any rapper you know: there's an unspoken rule of studio etiquette that encourages you to never be the last person writing. But if you do find yourself in that position, you'd better have an amazing verse by the end of it.

Thirty minutes after starting I was finally done and ready to record.

If the writing process was swift, the recording process was even faster. It quickly became evident that I was dealing with professionals. This excited the hell out of me. These guys weren't just giving up quick, throwaway verses. They had produced well-thought-out lyrics that included the kind of intricate wordplay utilized by my favorite mainstream rappers.

On the outside I was doing a pretty good job holding down my excitement as I handled the engineering responsibilities, but on the inside I was going nuts. I did my best to be the engineer and producer for them that John had been for me. I was honest, constructive, and detailed with my suggestions. And although they probably didn't really need my direction, they appreciated my willingness to be honest.

Hearing these lyricists record such clean verses over my beat made J.O. and I raise the bar on our own verses. When it was J.O.'s turn to record, he took just a few takes. I went next, still geekin' off the energy of the room, and I vowed to get it done just as fast as everyone else. When I recorded a take that I was satisfied with I began mixing the song. About forty-five minutes later the entire track was mixed and completed.

We played that song continuously, maybe twenty times over the next hour. We ended up creating a banger we called "The D.A. Anthem." (D.A. was short for Del Amo, which was the section of Carson where we all lived.) At the end of the session we exchanged emails and congratulatory fist bumps. Before leaving, Ghrimm pulled me off to the side to express his gratitude for opening my home to him and his squad. He said he specifically appreciated the freedom and ease he felt recording with me. As he walked to his car he turned back and asked if I'd be down to link up again.

I agreed without hesitation.

808S AND TEN-MINUTE FL STUDIO DRILLS

Over the next few weeks I was flying high off of that session and the buzz "The D.A Anthem" was starting to gain locally. And the more Ghrimm and I connected for sessions, the more we became an inseparable musical duo. To our surprise, we found out we had a lot of things in common. For starters, we both shared a genuine love for experimental music and rap groups like Outkast. We both had families from the south, which caused us to speak with strong southern accents. But most importantly, Ghrimm and I were both rappers and producers who used FL Studio to make our beats.

I've never met anyone who loved the sub bass of an 808 quite like Ghrimm. When he played me the beats he was working on, the bass was so heavy it made me squint my eyes. Before John made his exit, he'd blessed my studio with a pair of M-Audio BX8a monitors, the low end of which was already disrespectful at low volume—so can you imagine how they sounded when Ghrimm pressed "play" on his 808-driven beats at *max* volume?

Working with Ghrimm forced me to become a more efficient producer and writer. He worked fast because he believed that the special moments in music happen when you keep moving and revise later. To reinforce this, he came up with a game called the

"Ten-minute FL Studio Drill." The rules were simple: one-at-a-time, for ten minutes only, we worked on a beat from scratch. When those ten minutes were up we had to click save and hand the console over to the next guy so he, too, could start a beat from scratch.

We did this for one to two hours every time we linked up. After a few months of practicing these drills, my beat-making process improved dramatically. As you can probably imagine, ten minutes isn't a very long time to complete a beat. You don't have much time while you're playing the game to question or second guess your decisions—you just have to shut up and keep moving! But ten minutes is more than enough time to get your ideas out and create something that has the potential to be special.

> *Ghrimm believed that the special moments in music happen when you keep moving and revise later.*

The game turned me into a monster of productivity. The simple practice of doing less thinking and more moving turned me into the beast many people applaud me for being today. To this day, artists marvel at how quickly I create my beats. And whenever I hear that compliment it takes me back to a simpler time when it was just Ghrimm and me with those ten-minute FL Studio drills.

When we weren't doing our speed drills, Ghrimm and I worked on finishing his new solo album. Since we were already working with one another he asked me if I'd be down to produce a few beats for it. At the time, Ghrimm was signed to an independent label called Street Beat Entertainment, with whom he did the majority of his recording. Ghrimm was labelmates with Young Magic, Agent J, and an artist named Ab-Soul.

MY INTRODUCTION TO AB-SOUL

Ghrimm often brought up Ab-Soul's name in our studio sessions.

Ab was also one of the artists J.O. had mentioned I should check out. At this point I still hadn't met him; all I knew about Ab-Soul was that he had an almost mythical reputation in Carson as an incredibly talented lyricist.

When I finally gave Ab's music a listen I was blown away. It sounded polished, witty, and sharp. Lyrically he reminded me of a young, *Reasonable Doubt* Jay-Z. What seemed incredible was that he was creating his music at about my age and in my neighborhood. At just twenty, Ab-Soul sounded like a seasoned veteran. I had to meet the dude and see him in action.

Little did I know that the opportunity was already on its way.

After months of recording at his label's studio, Ghrimm decided to start recording his album at mine. Because we'd been spending so much time together we had developed a really solid chemistry and workflow. Our sessions started mirroring that first one when we did "The D.A. Anthem."

One day as Ghrimm finished laying a verse on a song he said he'd like Ab-Soul to feature on it.

When he asked me if it would be okay to have Ab-Soul come to my studio to record his verse, all I could reply with was a huge "HELL, YEAH!" The idea of having both Ghrimm and Ab-Soul rapping over one of my beats was mind-blowing.

I'll never forget the first day Ab-Soul came to my studio. Anybody with an ounce of foresight could already see this guy was going to be a major deal in the industry. Even if he hadn't achieved the astronomical heights of success he has today, I'd still never forget him. Ab-Soul did something in the studio that day that I've only ever seen Jay-Z do (in his documentary, *Fade to Black*). More on that in a minute.

Things started pretty much like any other day off from work for me. I did some minor straightening up in the studio to get rid of the disgusting smell of sandwich meats that had clung to my clothes from my job the night before. Then I booted up my desktop computer and went to work.

About 11:00 a.m. I got a call from Ghrimm saying he was on his way and that Ab-Soul was close behind. I opened the session for the song Ghrimm wanted Ab on and started making minor tweaks to it. In that moment I felt the pressure weighing on my shoulders to produce *results*.

> *Around this time there were a lot of sessions where I didn't know what the hell I was doing. But what I lacked in experience I made up for in tenacity, hunger, and eagerness to find the answers. My go-to response to a problem was, "I'll figure it out."*

Truth be told, around this time there were a lot of sessions where I didn't know what the hell I was doing. But what I lacked in experience I made up for in tenacity, hunger, and eagerness to find the answers. My go-to response to a problem was, "I'll figure it out." In those days I put a lot of pressure on myself to produce results. I was hungry for success and wanted to be prosperous beyond my wildest imagination. But that wasn't going to happen if I couldn't produce results in the presence of professionals.

Ghrimm arrived earlier than expected. I started showing him the changes I'd made to his song, but before we reached the chorus he got the call that Ab was outside.

My patio was at the back of our house, so I had to walk my guests through the dining room. This was where my grandpa usually sat watching television at an insane volume because he was hard of hearing. Lucky for me, he rarely complained about the volume of my music because he could barely hear it. Besides, I think he was more concerned about the character of the guests I'd invited than with the noise being made.

I could always tell how easy or difficult it was going to be to work with my guests simply by how they said hello to my grandpa. If they gave him a warm, genuine greeting, most times we had an amazing and productive session. If it was short and dismissive, the session would usually be a migraine to deal with.

I opened the front door and there was Ab-Soul wearing his infamous black shades. I playfully yelled out, "Soul!" to which he gave me a very formal, "Curtiss King, what's the word?"

I led him through the dining room towards the patio, but not without the "Grandpa Test."

He was one of the first artists to shake my grandfather's hand, also adding, "A genuine pleasure to meet you, sir."

From that encounter alone I figured we were in for a great session.

Ghrimm and Ab-Soul exchanged small talk as I prepared my multitrack program—Adobe Audition—for recording. Ghrimm explained to Ab the concept of the song to give him some direction for his feature. Ab didn't say much back; he just nodded his head. I played the song once through for Ab to get a feel for it, and his only reaction was "Dope." Then he asked me to loop around the section he was supposed to record over.

> *I could always tell how easy or difficult it was going to be to work with my guests simply by how they said hello to my grandpa.*

My heart was beating like crazy. I was already nervous about having to deliver as an amateur engineer and producer on Ghrimm's album, but this session really increased the pressure. What's more, Ab's serious demeanor made it a lot less creatively loose of an environment than what I was accustomed to. It was clear he wasn't here to play games.

I was definitely out of my creative comfort zone.

Ab hadn't come with a pen and pad to write his verse. Remember when Jay-Z gave us a rare, behind-the-scenes glimpse into his recording process in the *Fade to Black* documentary? Remember how he sat alone in the corner of the studio and mumbled what sounded like gibberish to himself while a beat looped in the background?

Remember how in a time span where most people couldn't finish an elementary-level crossword puzzle, Jay-Z wrote an entire song in his head without the assistance of a pen and pad?

I remember watching this and thinking to myself that the guy was a freak of nature. I'd never witnessed anyone retain and recite that many original lyrics without the assistance of a pen and pad.

Until I met Ab-Soul.

Me: "Yo, do you need a pen and pad, fam?"

Ab-Soul: [smiles] "Nah, I'm good bro, but thank you."

The beat looped around for at least ten minutes, and all the while my anxiety grew. *What if he doesn't like my beat? What if it's difficult to write to? What if he looked at my cheap studio equipment and had second thoughts about recording here?* I didn't know what was going on.

Meanwhile, Ghrimm didn't seem bothered at all.

I tried to keep myself busy checking my Myspace page and text messages. After another five minutes I was running out of ideas to distract myself from my anxiety, so I decided to text Ghrimm, hoping he could shed some light on what was happening.

Me: Yo, do you think he's feeling the song? Is he writing?

Ghrimm: Don't trip. WATCH.

Don't trip? Watch? What the hell did that mean?

But I followed his instructions, and about three minutes later Ab stood up and said:

"I'm ready; let's run it."

I was confused about what was happening. Nevertheless, I nodded my head, stood up to adjust the microphone to his height, sat back down in my desk chair and moved my mouse to an open channel. I asked Ab to do a mic check; he put his headphones on and repeated to himself:

"I'm Ab-Soul, and I'm real at this rap shit."

After repeating this five or six more times he looked at me, still sporting his shades, and said, "Run it."

Take one, he rapped his verse about halfway, stopped, and mumbled again, "I'm Ab-Soul and I'm real at this rap shit."

Take two, he delivered his verse through to the end. I sat there in utter disbelief. Ab had an intricate see-saw delivery where he'd take these unexpected pauses in between his lyrics then cap them off with a crazy punchline. Following the rhyming patterns in his flow was like trying to follow a Miles Davis trumpet solo—you don't know where it's going next, but it sounds right wherever it lands.

Ab asked how Ghrimm felt about his second take. Ghrimm responded with a confident, "YES." Ab then asked me what I thought, and something about the way he asked led me to believe he wanted to do another take. I said I thought it was fire, but we could always save it and do another take. He thought for a second, put the headphones back on his head and said, "Let's run it back." Like clockwork, he mumbled, "I'm Ab-Soul and I'm real at this rap shit."

Take three: THAT take was the one. It felt right.

Ab proceeded to record a few ad-libs, and then just like that he said he had to leave for his 9-5 at the record store.

I walked Ab to the front door, saying, "I greatly appreciate you coming through to record, bro. I've never recorded with anybody that sounded like that. You killed it. Thank you again, man."

"It's nothing," he said. "I'm digging your production. Let's link again and create."

I appreciated his props, but I wasn't sure if it was just the usual talk rappers exchange with one another when departing. Either way, we exchanged contacts and promises to work together in the near future.

Little did I know that not only would we meet up again in the next two weeks, but we would continue to work with each other for the next eleven years.

AB-SOUL SIGNS TO TDE

I worked miracles on my days off from my sandwich job. My sessions with Ghrimm helped me work at a faster pace creatively, so I ended up getting more music done for both of us on my days off. All the fun we were having made me dread going back to my draining-ass job. But anticipating our next session also made work fly by as I daydreamed about beats I could produce for Ghrimm—and now Ab-Soul.

On one of my Mondays off I went out on a limb and texted Ab to see if he'd be down to create some music. Unfortunately, he had to work that day, but he was still open to us creating on his next day off. That turned out to be the following Thursday—which I also had off— and I was HYPED. I decided to create some brand-new beats specifically for him.

In the mid 2000s I was still bumping Jay-Z's *The Black Album* heavily. On a random Internet search that Monday I stumbled on a handful of acapellas from *The Black Album*. The Ab-Soul and Jay-Z comparison was something I just couldn't get over. I would come to learn that Ab-Soul was actually a huge fan of Jay-Z. With this in mind, I thought I should build a beat for Ab centered around a classic Jay-Z acapella line. (Mind you this was before we heard Cassidy drop a song with a similar idea called "I'm a Hustla," which sampled a Jay-Z acapella from "Dirt Off Your Shoulder.")

I didn't think it was a very innovative idea, just that it'd be super trippy to hear an older Jay-Z on the hook of a song with a rapper who sounded like a younger Jay-Z. After skimming through Jay-Z lines I found the perfect phrase to sample from his song "Public Service Announcement":

I get my "by any means" on whenever there's a drought.
Get your umbrellas out because that's when I brainstorm

I chopped the sample up in FL Studio, dropped it into the FL Slicer, found a suitable tempo, and began building drums around it. The drums led to some synthesizers and the synths led to a bassline. About two hours later I finished, exported the beat, and emailed it to Ab.

Me: Yo, Ab, I just sent you a beat to check out, let me know what you think.
[ten minutes later:]
Ab-Soul: Aye, this sounds crazy. I'll be there on Thursday to record it.

I read that text with the biggest smile on my face. Thursday rolled around and, as promised, Ab came by with the song completed. The following week I cooked up some more ideas and we did the same thing.

When I sessioned up with Ghrimm and Ab-Soul in those days, it wasn't about money—it was all about the music. My sandwich job gave me the luxury to take chances on myself and others. Like I said earlier, I hated that job, but I also loved it for allowing me to be my own angel investor. It was also the thorn in my side that I needed as a reminder to go even harder on my days off.

After months of working with Ab-Soul we started to build a solid relationship as peers and homies. He was a stand-up guy even back then. (Now, almost eleven years later, he's still the same way.) He became a Carson legend at a very young age because he represented

> *When I sessioned up with Ghrimm and Ab-Soul in those days, it wasn't about money—it was all about the music. My sandwich job gave me the luxury to take chances on myself and others.*

Carson in a major way. So, you can imagine the excitement we had in the city when the word got around that he'd signed to Top Dawg Entertainment.

During the months Ab and I were working together he gave me hints that he might part ways with his original label. I never asked him about it because I felt it wasn't any of my business. Not to mention, I was more concerned about creating music.

One day Ghrimm called and told me Ab was officially parting ways with his label. A few weeks later I sent Ab a text that didn't directly refer to his departure but which just let him know that my studio was forever open to him no matter what he wanted to work on. About five minutes later I got a phone call.

In a very Ab-Soul-ish, nothing-but-the-facts way he explained to me his situation and a new opportunity he had in the works.

"It's not official yet," he said, "but it's looking like I'm about to be rocking with TDE."

I said, "Oh, word?! Congrats, bro!"

"I appreciate that, and the last few months of us working. I want to repay you for your hospitality."

"Not a problem, bro, it was my pleasure. What's up?"

"Well, you know TDE has Jay Rock and K.Dot right?"

"Yeah. Both of them are dope."

"Make me a CD of your *best* beats and I'll float it around the studio when I go over there."

I couldn't believe my ears. "Are you serious? I got you. Thank you, Soul."

"My dude. Holler at you soon."

I had no idea just what would come of that phone conversation or of my decision to burn that CD full of my best beats, but of course I hoped it would represent the next level in my career as a producer. At the time, Jay Rock was one of the biggest artists emerging on the West Coast and K.Dot (better known now as Kendrick Lamar) was touring right alongside him. I wasn't even sure if my beats were ready for that level. These doubts felt very real to me; I saw myself as a local producer without credits.

> **My hunger for more was stronger than my fear of failing.**

But it didn't matter. This was a golden opportunity, and my hunger for more was stronger than my fear of failing. I compiled a CD that same night, filled to capacity with twenty of my best beats. The next morning, I met Ab-Soul at his job and hand-delivered the CD. I thanked him again for the opportunity. He simply smiled and said, "You're welcome."

I drove home HYPED at the possibilities attached to that exchange. At work I dreamed about what Jay Rock would sound like over my production. I washed the dishes imagining K.Dot running lyrical laps around my beats. Sure, I was letting my imagination run wild, but I put a lot of hope into that CD circulating around their studio. I thought this was going to be my big break.

For the next few months those dreams seemed bound to stay just that: dreams. That was my first taste of the reality of the music industry. Nothing moved as fast as it seemed to in those rapper biopics.

After I gave Ab the CD I didn't hear much from him. I found out later that as soon as he got signed to TDE they put him to work. We didn't speak again for several months. I'd text him from time to time to check in and all he could say was that they had him working like crazy, but he would loop me in soon.

Eventually those months turned into a year since I had officially hand-delivered that CD to him. I knew he was busy and I believed him when he said that he'd look out for me, but I secretly began to become disappointed in myself.

Did I choose the wrong beats? Were those beats wack? What if Jay Rock heard them, thought they were garbage and now has a permanent bad taste in his mouth when my name gets brought up?

At the time all these thoughts felt legitimate to me because I didn't understand the inner workings of the music business.

As consumers—even as musicians—looking at the industry from the outside, we don't always have a sense of what's going on with an artist and his or her label. The end product we purchase and hold in our hands is usually the result of months or even years of hard work. In reality it's pretty standard for labels of TDE's caliber to be tight-lipped and cryptic about their process until the music is complete. TDE took their business and creative process very seriously. They calculated every move they made.

MY FIRST PLACEMENT: AB-SOUL & KENDRICK LAMAR

I had no idea of the inner workings of a successful independent rap label, so I just assumed my beats sucked and needed work. After almost a year and a half of doubt, working to improve my beats, and me eventually coming to grips with the reality that they weren't digging my beats, guess who I got a phone call from?

Ab had good news. He was just wrapping up his first official project under TDE; it was called *Longterm*. "What's good, Curtiss? Just wanted to give you a heads-up that we're using one of your beats on my debut. It came out crazy."

Ab called the song "Watch Yo Lady." He also added that the song featured his labelmate, K.Dot—better known today as *Kendrick Lamar*.

Now this may sound crazy and wildly Kanye-ish, but I was truthfully hoping to hear the news that Jay Rock was the surprise guest feature and not Kendrick. Those of you who were TDE fans around 2008 will understand why I felt that way. At that time, Jay Rock was one of the West Coast's brightest stars. His name was buzzing heavy and K.Dot was his young apprentice. On many occasions, K.Dot would fill in on tour as Jay Rock's hype man. But even back then when he was paying his dues early on, K.Dot was a lyrical swordsman. So I was still extremely grateful and excited that he was rapping on one of my beats. I knew he and Ab would kill it.

I thanked Ab for giving me the opportunity to be a part of his debut mixtape with TDE and said I couldn't wait to tell my friends and family the great news. But before the final words of that sentence came out my mouth, Ab stopped me. TDE, he said, did things very differently. He gave me strict instructions not to disclose the news about my placement or the album to the public. This came from the higher ups at the label. Of course, I agreed.

TDE kept their music and the business of their music shut off from the rest of the world until they were ready to share it. Nobody affiliated with TDE could say a thing to the public about future releases until TDE was ready. And even though I wasn't a part of TDE, that cutoff also applied to me.

This explained the year and a half where I knew absolutely nothing about my placement on Ab's album. The ball was always in TDE's court. I only knew what Ab felt he could tell me. I didn't even know what the song sounded like! If you think I'm exaggerating about this, I wasn't even able to *hear* the song until it was officially uploaded to the public on Ab-Soul's Myspace the day of the *Longterm* mixtape release!

Don't get me wrong. I'm not complaining about TDE's secretive ways; it was their business to run as they saw best. This was also the era when songs were leaked left and right before their release dates. I was just a young producer trying my best to get used to the process. My personal frustrations about any delays were, I felt, normal, but they were quickly drowned out by the level of excitement I felt with my first placement. It was difficult to keep silent, but I did, and Ab greatly appreciated that I kept my word.

PAYCHECK OR PAYING MY DUES?

All the producers reading this are probably wondering how much I got paid for my placement with Ab-Soul. Well, to be completely honest, I was never paid for that placement, or for any of the later placements I got with Ab-Soul & TDE.

I initially assumed this was because the first few albums for which I got placements were free projects that didn't generate much, if any, income for TDE. This was the pre-music streaming era and a time when downloads and ringtones reigned supreme. But even when Ab's streaming-era album, *Control System*, dropped in 2012 and went to #1 on the iTunes Hip Hop charts, I never pressed the issue of getting paid for my production on it. As far as I was concerned, I was paying my dues. The money I was missing out on was my personal tuition for a course in music industry politics 101. In fact, I never expected to be paid, so the conversation never came up.

There are probably some people out there who think I'm an idiot for letting that go. But I must encourage young producers to do as I did in these days: trust your intuition. It is important for you to be clear about your goals and not lose sight of your focus. At the time I wanted to get my name out there and work with a caliber of rappers that would attract more opportunity. Many people told me what *they* thought I should do. But I never gave a damn about that. When I look at the life and career I have today I realize the experience with TDE was way more important to me than a check would have been. I knew the money would come when I centered my focus on it, even if it wasn't from TDE, so I just kept paying my dues and learning my lessons. TDE paying me would have been icing on the cake, but I made the decision to be on the right side of history. You will also be faced with this decision as you begin your journey through the industry. You must not only understand that people will use your dreams against you, but you must be okay with it. Resiliency and laserlike focus are two important skills to develop as you march forward towards your dreams.

> *As far as I was concerned, I was paying my dues. The money I was missing out on was my personal tuition for a course in music industry politics 101.*

I cringe when I see producers publicly complain about famous rappers stealing their beats and not paying them for them. The fact that many of these producers willingly sent these beats to said rappers without any instructions on how they could or couldn't use them shows me how unfocused many of us are. Producers, KNOW WHAT YOU WANT. Even if it eventually changes, that's fine. Just make sure that you're deliberate with your movements. My placements with

Ab were investments in his career *and* my own. Given TDE's huge presence online and off, my placements were like a huge billboard for my beats on the 405 freeway.

SESSIONS AT TDE

In retrospect, too, I think that because I kept my word when the stakes were high, and because I focused on giving value instead of taking, I earned another level of respect from Ab—and to a certain degree from the higher-ups at TDE. My first placement was my "foot in the door" of the music business. After that I was invited to many of Ab's sessions in the following years to press play on my newest beats. Those sessions allowed me to build relationships with TDE members and leaders like Sounwave, Ali, Dave Free, Punch, Top, Kendrick, Jay Rock, and eventually ScHoolboy Q. I knew my place and I never tried to get in the way when I got invited to the studio. I was awkward and quiet around them because the opportunity was intimidating. Even before TDE rose to the stratospheric levels of success and fame it has today I remember thinking in those sessions: *These guys are going to be HUGE one day.*

Most of the time I didn't feel like I fit into their circle because I was such a square back then. I felt like the least talented person in the room. But I was always inspired to be greater when I was in their presence. I'd look around and ask myself, *How the hell did I get here and, more importantly, how can I STAY?*

This behind-the-scenes peek into the early days of TDE still inspires me. Everyone there moved like a championship-bound football team. They had rules on the wall that reminded them to stay disciplined and above the nonsense. They had extensive archives of music that most of us will never get to hear. They worked hard for everything they have today.

Those studio sessions made me make a few personal commitments to myself when in the presence of musicians more talented than myself:

- Be the easiest person to work with.
- Be the best I can be at following directions the first time.
- Stay out of the way.
- Don't be on social media bragging about where I'm at.
- Don't request pictures or autographs.
- Don't be a distraction to the creative flow.
- Deliver creatively when called upon.
- Speak only if I feel I can offer value.
- Use my sense of humor to my advantage.

I think this mindset is why I kept getting invited back, and the payoff was incredible. One afternoon visit I found myself making a beat for Kendrick. Another I made a beat for ScHoolboy Q and recorded him so late that I ended up spending the night in the studio. I remember waking up the next morning when Ab walked in and asked me if I wanted to make a cameo in a video he was shooting. I literally

> *TDE still inspires me. Everyone there moved like a championship-bound football team. They had rules on the wall that reminded them to stay disciplined and above the nonsense. They worked hard for everything they have today.*

spent twenty-four hours in the TDE studio that day witnessing how hard they work. It was my first time being in a studio environment where someone was always recording. Me just being there and down to help whenever I could presented me with countless opportunities.

Eventually one of those opportunities came knocking when Ab began working on his follow up project to *Longterm*, appropriately titled *Longterm 2*.

LONGTERM 2

Producers, it's not just a matter of opening the door when opportunity comes knocking. You need to anticipate her arrival and make the appropriate preparations. When I chose to learn graphic design, I did it because I needed that tool to get things done in my career. Every hour I spent on YouTube watching Photoshop tutorials was absolutely necessary for me to accomplish my goals. I've always had a go-getter mentality. I often told myself that if I couldn't afford to pay somebody to do something for me, I couldn't afford not to learn how to do it myself. This was a way of life for me, and little did I know this was the equivalent of me straightening up my living room for the arrival of a visit from a lady named opportunity.

One night Ab-Soul invited me to TDE to listen to the finished version of a new song I'd produced. This was a rare opportunity for an outsider like me to get an insider's point of view. This was also the first time I met the TDE engineer, Ali. Ali, like Ab, wasn't a man of many words; in fact, I remember thinking at the time, *How can they possibly communicate like this during sessions?*

I had the title track to *Longterm 2*, and I couldn't believe it. But in truth every song Ali played off the album sounded amazing. All the work Ab had done after signing with TDE had made him an even sharper lyricist and songwriter. He no longer sounded like a young Jay-Z—he sounded like an older, more experienced and seasoned Ab-Soul.

After Ali played the last song, Ab and I talked about the direction of the album. Ab explained that the release process for this album would be a lot faster than the one for the first *Longterm*. He felt *LT2* would be his biggest album to date. TDE was getting a substantial push behind it so he was doing his best to prepare and perfect his final product. Then he mentioned he was having an issue with his graphic designer about getting the album cover done.

Opportunity: Knock, Knock

Me: Please come in, Miss Opportunity.

My mind raced a million miles a second. *Should I ask him if he needs me to make his album cover? Would he allow me or even trust me to do it justice?*

Before I could even think of a rebuttal to talk myself out of it, the words came pouring out:

Me: "If you need an album cover, I can make you one."

Ab-Soul: "That's right, I forgot you do your own graphic work. I'm with it. Let me just run it by Dave."

My heart was lodged uncomfortably in my throat and my foot was twitching eagerly in the direction of my mouth.

What are you doing Curtiss? Do you really think you have what it takes to make cover art for an album this important?

My honest answer was this: *I don't know, but I'm more afraid of NOT trying to do it.*

For the next twenty-four hours, the *LT2* album cover was the only thing I worked on. One of the higher ups at the label—Dave—sent me a few photos and notes giving brief directions which I kept in mind while I worked. The next day I sent him about six versions of the album cover. A few hours later he expressed appreciation for my work and asked me to make a few minor changes to one of the versions. That version ended up becoming the official album cover for *LT2*. Ab called me the next day and expressed his gratitude—not only for me doing it, but for getting it done fast.

BEING THE BASS

Although I knew I didn't fit in with TDE, a part of me still wanted to be signed to their label. But God had different plans for my career and he put them in my life for a solid reason. Those gentlemen at TDE gave me my first real experience of seeing how a well-oiled machine operates in the music business. And not just any machine, but one of the best that Hip Hop has ever seen. TDE gave me my first legitimate start in this business and for that I am forever grateful.

I often used to think about how a kid like me made it so far from his Carson patio. Here I was producing the title track for one of the biggest artists in his city *and* creating his album cover. To this day, I chalk all that up to me moving as the bass does in a beat: patiently, consistently and in an omnipresent fashion—I was just always there. If the bass is truly the direct vibration of the soul, then I could hear what my soul wanted to do: *create more opportunities.* Over the years, I have learned that I have the heart of an artist. Yes, I am a producer, I am a rapper, I am a video editor, and I am a graphic designer. But most importantly I am an artist. Artists create. Artists use what they must to the best of their ability and create things that leave audiences asking how they did it.

That's our job as Prosperous Producers.

Lessons to Take Away from Chapter 8

1. Never allow your environment to limit the vision you have for your dreams.

2. Collaborate with a producer who makes the process exciting.

3. Ten-minute FL Studio drills trained me to be the professional I am today. Keep practicing and honing your craft so you're ready whenever opportunity arrives.

4. Seek to work with other producers and artists even (especially) if they are more talented than you.

5. Invest in the artists you believe in early on and reap the benefits when they achieve success.

6. The music business is a slow-moving machine; have patience with the process.

7. Carefully weigh what you're getting for your work—sometimes experience is at least as valuable as money.

8. Don't be afraid to speak up when you feel like you have value to offer.

CHAPTER 9

STRUCTURE
THE BEAT

"We don't just make beats—we provide scores for movies that haven't been made yet. So every time I open up FL I ask myself, what scene in the movie is this going to be for?"

~ Willie B (TDE Producer)

Structuring or composing an instrumental is like getting your life in order. When most producers make beats, they have a general idea of the direction they'd like to take their beat, but along the way the process takes a few unexpected twists and turns. Maybe a beat you're working on started as a trap anthem, but after doing some instrument digging you come across a snare drum that instantly transforms it into something Hip Hop—and this changes your mind entirely about its final destination.

My life has been just as unpredictable as the beats I've made in it.

Writing this book is causing me to reminisce about some very tough periods. I am truly lucky to be the man I am today after traveling the route I did.

I've talked a lot about mentors along my path, but much of the time I've actually been going alone, and this has often made my journey a lonely one. I had so many opportunities to make the wrong decisions and lose it all. Of course, many of the choices I've had to make have affected my music career in positive and negative ways. Sometimes I made smart decisions, other times not so much.

Messing up my credit in my twenties?

Not saving at least ten percent of four-years' worth of earnings at my sandwich gig?

Quitting my job without saving enough money to survive for a few months?

Bad, bad, and bad.

Even my decision to chase placements for the first ten years of my career is questionable.

But *one* decision that kept me alive during my most turbulent times was my choice to *always readjust and reconstruct my path when I fell off.*

From my childhood through my late twenties, being broke was just a part of life. I wasn't lazy; I was just used to being broke even when I had a job. I put a lot of hope into my music career taking off, but after years and years of trying it just wasn't happening for me financially. It didn't help that I wasn't charging anyone for my musical services. Even after my first placement I didn't think about

> *One decision that kept me alive during my most turbulent times was my choice to always readjust and reconstruct my path when I fell off.*

charging people for my beats because I was still insecure about my worth.

However, things got real for my family and me in the mid-2000s. My dad and I still had a complicated relationship because I'd chosen to pursue music and not a degree. I tried to keep him posted on my accomplishments in music, but his often-lukewarm reactions made me feel like he was uninterested in hearing about it. Our relationship became a bit more fragmented at that time.

Also, around 2007 my mom lost her job and had to take care of her aging parents full time. Unfortunately, within a year both my grandfather and grandmother passed away. This left a tremendous amount of stress and debt on my mom's shoulders.

On top of this, I had quit my sandwich gig months before when they'd refused to give me more hours.

My mom made miracles happen in our kitchen when we had very little to eat. We spent a lot of time going through the embarrassing ritual of dumping coins into the Coinstar machine at the supermarket just to be able to buy a few chili cheese dogs from Wienerschnitzel. Our financial situation caused us both a tremendous amount of stress. Eventually this led to loud arguments between the two of us. I know now (and probably knew even then) that most of the time I was in the wrong in our arguments, even if I didn't want to admit it. My dreams to pursue music were MY dreams, and the people in my life hadn't asked to go on that journey with me. They also hadn't asked to become angel investors for my dream.

So as time went on part of me started to feel guilty when I made music with the homies for free. The fact was that without a job or a solid plan for monetization I had no business doing free work for ANYBODY. Not even my friends. It was time to do something about it.

As you can imagine, I struggled with the thought of having that conversation. How do you tell the friends you've been recording for free for months that you now have to charge them to record and to use your beats? Friends who've supported you since you weren't even a fraction of the talent you've become? I often wondered if asking them for money was worth losing our friendship over.

Eventually I realized that all of my questions were rooted in my own insecurity. I was scared to charge my friends because I thought they would stop being my friends because of it. But in truth, if they were really my friends they'd understand, even if they did feel a certain way about paying.

So after some deep soul searching I knew what I had to do. Life around me was financially unraveling and I really had little choice anyway. I decided to move forward on my decision to charge my friends.

Those were some of the hardest conversations I've ever had. As it turned out, of all the friends with whom I had this conversation, Ghrimm was the only one who actually stuck around and paid me for my services. Most of my other friends understood why I was asking but they just didn't have the money. I also understood where they were coming from, but I had to do what I had to do.

I charged Ghrimm $25 for a beat and he paid for two. That's just the type of man he was. If he supported you it was going to be unconditional support. Ghrimm gave me my first taste of what it felt like to be compensated for my work as a music producer. For that I am forever thankful.

GOODBYE CARSON, HELLO INLAND EMPIRE

In 2009, after what I *thought* would be the most difficult financial stretch of my life, my mother received money from my grandfather's will. When she received the money she was ready to leave Carson. She had her eyes set on moving fifty miles north to the Inland

Empire—more specifically to Rancho Cucamonga, where the cost of living was significantly lower. About a month later she found a townhome for rent that she fell in love with, and she sold the house in Carson.

I too was ready to say goodbye to the home I'd grown up in and the city that had raised me. I was ready to say goodbye to my patio studio, which had offered me my first taste of creative freedom. I was even ready to say goodbye to my friends and prepare for the official reconstruction of the twenty-fifth year of my life.

In other words, moving was bittersweet, but I was excited and ready for the opportunity to start over in the Inland Empire.

The townhome was beautiful, but not as beautiful as the smile on my mother's face. This move represented a fresh start for her as well. She decked that townhome out something special. She bought new furniture and paintings that were perfectly color-coordinated. I had a bedroom with an actual bed and dresser for the first time since high school. The only drawback was that the neighboring townhomes were extremely close to us. This would make it a challenge to create my music without wearing headphones.

> **Moving was bittersweet, but I was excited and ready for the opportunity to start over.**

I didn't know much about the people or my new surroundings in Rancho, but I figured that in a new city, Curtiss King Beats had a clean slate. Nobody would expect any free work because they were the homey. At least, that's how I envisioned it. When we first moved to the IE, I made a promise that any relationship I built through music would be business *first*.

The only problem was that I didn't know anyone yet. The Inland Empire forced me to fully break out of my hermit, homebody ways.

After all, if I was going get my name out there I knew I'd have to physically get out of the house and meet people.

Seems like a rather simple task for Curtiss King, right?

Wrong. I arrived from Carson a very insecure and introverted young man. I still saw myself through the lens of someone not quite good enough. I still felt like less of a man for not being able to provide for myself or my family. And even though we were all in a better place financially in 2009, that insecurity still haunted me. I attempted to mask it with tattoos, fake glasses, and colorful sneakers that shifted the focus from what was going on inside me.

But in truth, in this new city I could be whoever I wanted to be, and I decided I wanted to be the King of Curtiss in a way that I'd never been before.

THE STORM ON MARS

My girlfriend at the time had been an IE native for years. She was a poet who was part of a spoken-word community called LionLike MindState. They were a loving artistic community that accepted me with open arms way before the Hip Hop community in the IE even knew who I was. It was because of LionLike MindState founder Judah 1 that I was able to throw a release party for my new album in a new city.

By 2009, I had a handful of albums and mixtapes to my name as the rapper Curtiss King. Each one of those albums taught me enough lessons that I could probably write another book about them after this one. Although the purpose of this book is to document my journey as a music producer, I'd like to take a second to share the influence that my journey as a rapper had on me as a music producer.

For me, creating an album as a rapper represents the ultimate freedom as a creative individual—especially when I'm the sole producer of the album. When I create an album for myself it's just me and the music. I'm able to access a freedom I'm not always able to access as a producer for other artists. When I'm creating a beat for a potential customer I have to create a balance between the things that I like and the needs of that customer. For example, I love creating beats with unpredictable drops and pauses, but I have to be considerate of the possibility that the potential customer may find these drops and pauses too difficult to rap over.

But when it's just me, the beat, and my recording software I'm free to take as many chances musically as I desire. I've actually made it a priority for each of my albums to purposely push the boundaries of my creativity—partly for fun and partly for growth. This may take the form of singing notes in an experimental style that takes me far out of my comfort zone, or of rapping over beats that are faster and more frantic than most beats I create with the intention of selling.

Keyden used to compare the album-making process to adding photos to a photo album. It was his philosophy that the songs we create, when recorded correctly, have the same nostalgic value as photos. So essentially a compilation of songs on an album is no different from a chronological collection of photos in an album. I agreed with this analogy. In fact, I agreed so strongly with it that I always made it my duty to create my albums around a theme or a specific period in my life, thinking that this way they'd feel more authentic and better stand the test of time.

> **For me, creating an album as a rapper represents ultimate freedom as a creative individual—especially when I'm the sole producer. When I create an album for myself it's just me and the music.**

However, I learned over the years that putting so much of myself into these albums exposed the good and not so glamorous parts of my life to complete strangers. And each time I willfully exposed my life to my audience through my albums it made me . . . nervous.

In March of 2009 I was incredibly nervous about my new album: *The Storm On Mars*. As I mentioned, I was a handful of albums into my own recording career at this point, but I still had doubts and insecurities as an artist, particularly about whether or not people would approve of my work.

To this day, I still feel goosebumps and jitters when I release new music. The only difference now is that I accept it as part of the process. This is true especially when you create music the way that I do: unbiased, unapologetic, brutally honest, and heartfelt. As artists and producers, when we showcase our own music to the public we really bear it all. In many ways we have a lot in common with exotic dancers—but we'll save that for another book.

> *To this day, I still feel goosebumps and jitters when I release new music. The only difference now is that I accept it as part of the process.*

So in the fall of 2009, I invited everyone I knew to my release party in the beautiful city of Diamond Bar. Myspace made it possible for me to befriend people in the community I'd never met in person. This was my first time throwing a show and I honestly had no idea what I was doing. What I *did* have experience in at this point was going to BAD shows, so I certainly knew what NOT to do.

I tried to treat the event in much the same way I treated the first time I taught myself how to make a beat. This meant making lists and approaching each step using common sense. First, I invited local jewelry and clothing vendors to set up their merchandise. I also invited the local DJ Cornbread to DJ for the night, along with a few of my artist homies from Carson to perform alongside some IE-based artists suggested by DJ Cornbread. My hope was that the show would attract opportunities for me to network and be exposed to the IE Hip Hop community.

The show went well, and thankfully two of the most influential figures in the IE Hip Hop scene came to it. Noa James and Lesa J were club promoters who threw a weekly event in Riverside called "The Common Ground." It was at a bar and grill called The Vibe, which was down the street from the University of California, Riverside. My girlfriend at the time had reservations about the venue because of the history of violence there, but this was where the Hip Hop was at, and I needed to be around that creative energy.

I thanked Noa and Lesa for coming out to my show and exchanged contacts with them. Not even a month later I got booked at their show as an artist. What I would quickly come to realize was that not only was Noa James a popular promoter in the IE but he was also a popular rapper in the area. He and Lesa also ran a website dedicated to showcasing independent artists and producers called BrickToYaFace.com.

THE COMMON GROUND

My first show at The Common Ground was met with a very *observant* response. The rappers who went on before me received loud screams and claps for their performances. I, on the other hand, received golf claps and cold stares as the audience studied my every word. I knew that this was an environment where rappers had to prove their worth in order to earn a reaction.

Unlike most rappers, this excited me! Seeing how loud they cheered for other rappers made me see the potential love an artist could receive.

I'd performed before—in Los Angeles. But there most shows were the same old story: an artist pouring his or her heart out to a crowd, only to receive little or no response at all from a jaded audience. You were a nobody to them unless a major *somebody* co-signed you.

But everything was different in the IE. They cared a lot less about the appearance of a rapper or who he knew and much more about his craft. The people in the IE were different as well, and I liked it. I started to feel like I'd fit in with them perfectly. They would listen in detail to what each live performer had to say and would make noise if they were impressed.

I thanked Noa and Lesa repeatedly for having me out to perform that night. I told them that if there was any way I could be a contributor to the scene I would.

Everyone was friendly to me that night, even if my performance only got a kind of lukewarm response. It was obvious that the people there *loved* Hip Hop. In one corner artists were freestyling in cyphers and in another they were sipping on brews and talking to the ladies. It was like the Hip Hop version of the TV show *Cheers*. The artists and people in attendance made it feel like a family reunion—full of family members I'd never met.

That night opened my eyes to the possibilities this new environment could offer me. I made plans to go back the following week strictly to network. I got business cards printed up and had a plan that I hoped would spread my name around fast as a producer.

> *I understood I was going to have to earn the right to spread my name around the IE. I would have to build myself up from scratch.*

FREE BEATS

I understood I was going to have to earn the right to spread my name around the IE. I would have to build myself up from scratch. I also knew that my biggest asset to my new community was my production. But I still had to ask myself: *How exactly do I get artists interested in **buying** beats from me?* I pondered this question for many of my first weeks in Rancho. One thing that came to me was this: no word in the English dictionary moves a product around faster than the word **FREE**.

Once I had this in mind a strategy just came to me:

- Offer your beat-making services for **FREE** to a handful of artists who are making significant noise in the area.
- Build **genuine** relationships with them.
- Make them **INCREDIBLE** beats and require each beat to include my beat tag.
- Offer them a **cut** of any beats I sell via their **referral**.
- After a few months, watch as my beats start to show up on multiple albums.

For a little while this strategy worked like a charm. I went to as many shows as I could afford to attend and scouted the next artist I wanted to invite over to work with me. I treated those artists like human beings and not potential dollar signs. I knew even then how important it would be for us to build together on an organic level.

Do you remember how I was initially hesitant to invite strangers over to my home to record music? Well, that was no longer an issue for me. I felt I had become a better judge of character when it came to what types of people I should and shouldn't invite over.

My first sessions in the IE were all during the daytime, when I was less likely to receive noise complaints from my neighbors. In fact, the only noise complaints I ever received were from my mom downstairs. She would frequently send me text messages asking me to turn the volume down.

Every artist I chose to work with had something special in my eyes. I didn't pick just anybody. I searched out artists who possessed great live-performance skills, made great beat selections, showcased an undeniable passion for their art, and carried themselves with humility when I spoke with them. After each show I attended, I scheduled a studio session for the following week. I tried my best to fill up my weeks.

Like clockwork, each artist came to my home studio on their assigned date and I produced an original beat for them on the spot. After about three weeks I started developing a routine for each session:

1. Ask the artist what they're currently working on.
2. Ask them what musical direction they want to go in.
3. Ask them to give me some examples of other rappers' songs that best represent their next direction.
4. Play them some of the beats I already have in my catalog that fit the style they're looking for.
5. Get to work.

Every session combined the lessons I'd learned up to that point in my producing career. If the rapper wanted me to chop a sample up for them I would reference my lessons from Victor. When a rapper wanted me to play something original I'd recall what John had taught me about chord progressions and staying in key. When a rapper only had a few hours to work with me in the studio I would immediately get into the mindset I was in when Ghrimm and I did our ten-minute FL Studio drills.

The variety of skills I exhibited in these sessions made for a lot of satisfied rappers. These artists created a word-of-mouth buzz for me in the area that, for a short time, was a tremendous boost for my business. The word around town was that a new producer named Curtiss King had a variety of fire beats for sale.

This buzz lasted for a few months and equated to a handful of sales, but unfortunately that initial wave eventually came to a screeching halt.

Although providing these beats for free was a great marketing tactic to draw in new artists, it also had some negative side effects. A lot of artists started approaching me expecting beats for free or for an unreasonable discount.

Scan the QR code to watch the Roscoe Da Taco video.

(When you watch my Roscoe Da Taco series on YouTube,[9] where I play the worst rap client ever, understand that much of that comedic material is from real life messages, emails, and requests I've received from rappers.)

But regardless of those few difficult customers, I had to push forward. I knew that if I wanted to make some sort of living selling my beats I was going to need to keep moving until an opportunity came around that would get people talking about my beats again.

It didn't take long for that, and it came in the form of a Myspace bulletin by Noa James that read:

ATTENTION ALL PRODUCERS: LAST DAY TO SIGN UP FOR THE KILL THAT NOISE BEAT BATTLE!

---

[9] Roscoe Da Taco: https://youtu.be/gVK6WY8WrXc

Lessons to Take Away from Chapter 9

1. Make wise financial decisions in your early years or pay for them later.
2. Sometimes you have to do it all yourself to attract the right kind of help.
3. Creatively use the word FREE to attract attention to your growing business.
4. Treat your business like a business: be professional, get yourself out there and get the work done.
5. Seek out the advantages to any new environment in which you find yourself.
6. Take creative musical chances on yourself so that you can grow as a music producer.

CHAPTER 10

MIX
THE BEAT

"It's good if you hear everything. It's great if you can see everything. It's perfect if you can feel everything."

~ THX (Producer)

B y far, the most common questions I receive from young music producers deal with the art of mixing. Some producers approach me confused about what constitutes a great mix and others are completely overthinking the process and repeatedly butchering their final beat.

Technically, mixing a beat is manipulating the volume and texture of each sound to create a more cohesive final product. Mixing to me has always been my chance to clearly translate the ideas of my often chaotic sound selection and arrangements to my audience without overwhelming them with what amounts to a pile of noise. Mixing for me is much like taking a picture on my cell phone and running it through multiple filters and edits until the viewer can see what I see. Or in the case of mixing a beat, it is my goal for my listener not only to hear what I am hearing, but as THX pointed out, to *feel* what I am feeling.

Mixing hasn't always been an easy journey for me. I have learned a lot thanks to my mentors and by making many personal errors over the years. As a matter of fact, I am still learning more and more about mixing. The older I get and the more I learn, the more I understand why producer Dr. Dre notoriously spent so many years tweaking his music before he released it. The old adage is true: the more you know, the more you owe. The more I have learned about mixing, the more energy I have wanted to give to the process. I don't think I'll ever stop learning—and I wouldn't have it any other way.

One of the most important lessons I've learned is that there is no wrong or right way to mix when your music is a direct reflection of your mind, heart, and body. Only you will know how accurately or inaccurately the sounds on the outside represent the sounds coming from within.

BEAT BATTLES AND BEAT SHOWCASES

Producers, say what you will about beat battles. You might argue they're biased and a waste of time, because music is not to be judged. You can complain about how the beats you hear in these competitions don't reflect REAL musicianship. You can complain about how REAL producers should spend their time pursuing placements instead of battling.

You can say whatever you like about beat battles—but I owe everything to them. They put my name on the map.

For producers who've never experienced a beat battle and don't quite know what one is, allow me to explain. A beat battle is generally a four-round competition between sixteen music producers in front of an audience and three judges. Rounds are generally head-to-head competitions where each producer takes a turn at playing a beat for a set amount of time, after which a winner is determined by the three judges—and/or by the crowd's approval. The last man standing walks away with cash and other prizes.

I've competed in at least fifteen beat battles over my career and each one was an intense adrenaline rush. There's no feeling like standing onstage next to an opponent who wants to absolutely demolish you with their production in front of a group of bloodthirsty music fanatics. I'd get a high every time they played a subpar beat that I knew I could destroy.

> *There's no feeling like standing onstage next to an opponent who wants to absolutely demolish you with their production in front of a group of bloodthirsty music fanatics.*

Beat battling can be maddening. For one thing, you can find yourself incredibly indecisive just when you need to be laser-focused. With each new beat that plays you second guess your next move. Sweat drips from your brow as you engage in an internal debate about which beat will obliterate your opponent. Do you play your best beat or risk saving it for the next round—if you're not eliminated by then? Beat battles are an intense sport, not for the faint of heart.

As I mentioned in the chapter on swing, in July of 2009, Noa James' and Lesa J's Kill That Noise beat battle was a big deal for producers in the area. KTN was also instrumental in pulling my business out of the slump it was in. At the time I had no idea how important it would be for me to join in. I couldn't predict that a beat battle would attract more artists to my beats. The way I saw it, it was well worth the $10 entry fee if I could play at least two beats for a crowd full of potential fans and customers.

Before then I hadn't had many opportunities to showcase my beats in front of strangers. The Internet gave me a taste of feedback from strangers, but nothing compared to what I encountered while playing a beat live before an unknown crowd.

Producers, listen to me clearly: your music may sound amazing in your own studio around your friends, but you don't TRULY know how tight you are until you play those same beats in front of a room full of unbiased individuals who have nothing to gain from you.

MY FIRST BEAT BATTLE

The first beat battle I competed in was in a Los Angeles bar in 2007. I lost in the first round because I didn't understand the rules of combat. I played to the level of my competition instead of playing to win my first round and thereby strike fear into the heart of my potential second-round opponent.

The next time I played my beats in front of a live audience of strangers was in 2008 at an event labeled a "beat cypher" at KAOS network in the legendary Leimert Park. I learned of the event from a random Myspace flier and decided to take a chance and go. At the showcase, there were at least twenty aspiring producers eager to jump onstage and let their beats bang. The flier said that each producer had about five minutes to play a few beats off their CD or flash drive. I spent an hour trying to figure out what beats to play.

When it was finally my time to go up my heart was pumping so loudly my voice was pulsating when I told the host what my producer name was. I played my beats, all the while looking down at the DJ equipment until I started hearing loud "ooooohs" and "ahhhs" from the crowd. The louder these chants became, the more I started to look up with confidence. When my set was complete I received handshakes and nods of approval—most notably from a producer by the name of Dibia$e.

KILL THAT NOISE

Now fast forward back to 2009 in the days just before the KTN beat battle (and before the beat battle where I competed against Captain, as discussed in "Chapter 4: The Swing"). As I was getting prepared, it became evident that beat battles were nowhere near as friendly as that beat cypher in 2008. I watched hours of YouTube footage from battles across the world after answering that Myspace bulletin posted by Noa. And I remembered my first defeat in 2007. I felt like I'd learned my lesson in that first battle, and I refused to lose like that again.

My first beat battle at the Kill That Noise competition I did what I set out to do: make my presence felt. I didn't go in expecting to win, only with the intention of playing as many beats as possible and showing the IE what I was working with.

I remember looking out into the crowd after playing each beat and seeing rappers mumbling lyrics to themselves. Rappers tapped my shoulder to take note of the title of each beat I played.

I thought to myself, *This is exactly where I need to be to raise proper awareness of my beats.*

And it was true. I needed this experience to grow my business and clientele. The best part about the excitement happening at that beat battle was that I didn't have to personally sell the rappers on my beats. The reactions of their peers all around them did that for me. That night, word-of-mouth officially caught fire again after my free beat campaign had burned down. Even though I lost the battle, I'd still made a substantial impact. Noa James and other notable figures in the IE wanted to work with me as a producer. What's more, it helped me break out of my shell.

Over the next few years that battle was the reason I hopped into many more battles in Southern California. The reaction I received from the crowds was like nothing I'd ever experienced. Battling became my new addiction. Once I met Captain, he introduced me to the theatrics of beat battles. By studying him I learned how to turn my battles into "must-see TV."

Like I said in the swing chapter, breaking out of my comfort zone to dance in front of these crowds was a huge accomplishment for me. When I was growing up I was known to be terrible at dancing, so I shied away from even trying. I'd always felt awkward and stupid when I danced.

But when I did it in beat battles I didn't feel that way. I moved differently because I *felt* differently. People even seemed to like the fact that I was different. I wasn't just a machine producing beats, but a likeable human being who wanted to have fun and who wasn't afraid of embarrassing himself. And another thing I think they appreciated: Captain taught me that when you move your hands to illustrate certain hits in your beats—say a particular snare or hi-hat patter—you open up your world to your audience.

So competing in beat battles helped me build relationships with artists and potential customers. But it also helped me create relationships with more experienced producers. One of these—whose name I've already mentioned above—I saw very often in these beat battles: the legendary Dibia$e.

> *Competing in beat battles helped me build relationships with artists, potential customers and more experienced producers.*

DIBIA$E

When we think of monsters in movies and fairytales, we usually picture snarling, menacing creatures with sharp teeth. Adjectives like "nice" and "humble" are probably the last ones you'd use if I asked you to describe your version of a monster. But in the case of the legendary Dibia$e, as a producer he's one of the nicest *monsters* you could ever meet.

When it came to making beats, Dibia$e was a BEAST in every sense of the word. If you were competing in a beat battle and you heard your named announced as Dibia$e's next opponent, you pretty much knew your evening was about to come to an end. Dibia$e reminded me of a West Coast J. Dilla. From the swing in his drums to his erratic use of vocal chops and eccentric arrangements, it was obvious that Dilla was one of his major influences. But Dibia$e was a true original, and also one of the kindest and most encouraging producers I've ever met. In fact, his kindness often made you forget that he was a stone-cold killer in beat battles.

Not many wanted it with Dibia$e—but I did. In my eyes he represented the top of the beat-battle throne. He was the West Coast champion of one of the nation's biggest beat battles, which was sponsored by Red Bull. The Red Bull Big Tune was thrown once a year, tournament style, in every major city.

The first time I battled Dibia$e was at a terribly orchestrated event where the final round consisted of six producers playing their beats back-to-back to determine a winner. Now, if you've ever experienced a beat battle you understand how hard it can be to judge even *two* contestants at a time. So try judging *six* producers and their *twelve* beats, all in the same round! Most of the judges couldn't even remember what the earlier beats in the round sounded like.

So it was terrible, but there was nothing I could to do about it. The only reason it was done that way was because the bar wanted to shut the show down at midnight and it was starting to run over. This prompted the promoter to rush everything so a winner could be determined.

I was pissed off at the lack of professionalism, but I was also excited at the prospect of finally competing against the legendary Dibia$e. To stay focused and above the shenanigans I kept reminding myself about my one goal at hand: beating Dibia$e. What better way to make a name for myself?

But it wasn't meant to be. This particular battle just so happened to have judges who were past victims of a Dibia$e thrashing. Dibia$e was killing everybody that night but only receiving lukewarm responses from the bitter judges. In the final six-man round, Dibia$e got voted out first.

Technically this meant that I beat Dibi, but it felt cheap, and my pride wouldn't allow me to count it as a win. I still wanted my chance to go head-to-head with him.

As for me, I lost to the remaining producers. All in all it had been a long night that I would've likely chalked up as a complete waste of time had it not brought me one step closer to building a friendship with Dibia$e. At the end of the night, he did something that most producers with his reputation would never do. He walked up to me and gave me the most heartfelt respect and encouragement for the beats I'd played.

> **At the end of the night, Dibia$e did something that most producers with his reputation would never do. He walked up to me and gave me the most heartfelt respect and encouragement for my beats.**

The more I talked to him the less I wanted to beat him. He was such a nice guy. I just wanted to give the man a hug. I was truly touched that somebody of his stature was showering my music with such praise. Before we left for the night we exchanged contacts and promises to link up. I left feeling inspired . . . but still wanting to go head-to-head with him.

My chance would come soon enough.

CURTISS KING VS. DIBIA$E

Ask and you shall receive, young Curtiss King!

A few months after exchanging contacts with Dibia$e, I finally got my chance to battle him on my home turf in the IE. In the months since our last battle I'd developed a reputation as a beat-battle bully (in a good way). I was winning left and right all-across Southern Cali. In anticipation of each battle I would work all week on new beats. I'd handpick samples from cartoons and TV themes directly off YouTube to use in my beats. It was important that I picked something people would recognize because it was part of my strategy to immediately connect with the audience.

When I found the right sample I proceeded to chop it up and lace it with my signature drums. Every single beat I created in the week preceding a battle was designed with one goal in mind: to embarrass my competition. And if I couldn't flat-out embarrass them I just planned to knock them off their "A" game by making them adjust to whatever I played. In fact, it didn't matter to me whether the judges picked me to win; my goal was to make my competition use their best beats out of respect for me as a competitor.

Those tactics generally had a high success rate with new competitors. But they meant nothing when I faced a seasoned competitor like Dibia$e. The week before *that* battle I specifically prepared beats for him just in case we crossed paths. To be honest, I wasn't even thinking about any of my other potential competitors— my mind was set on a battle with Dibia$e.

The stars seemed to be in perfect alignment that night. Dibia$e and I coasted through our first rounds and awaited the announcement of who we'd be competing against in the second; sure enough Dibia$e and I were called. I heard murmers of "Uh-oh" rippling through the audience. This was the battle everyone was hoping to see that night. I was finally getting my shot at Dibia$e.

I approached the round with an all-or-nothing attitude. I didn't care if I lost. I just wanted the opportunity to show my peers that I could handle my own versus a legend like Dibia$e.

The first beat I played was a sample of the popular Nickelodeon show *Guts*, and the crowd reaction was loud. This didn't bother Dibia$e at all. In fact, he just stood off to the side, calmly nodding his head to the beat as he awaited his turn.

> *I approached the round with an all-or-nothing attitude. I didn't care if I lost. I just wanted the opportunity to show my peers that I could handle my own versus a legend like Dibia$e.*

Dibi's first beat out the gate was an absolute banger. The crowd got even louder. When the beat ended, you could feel the tension in the room building as he contemplated what to play next. And on his second beat, Dibia$e sent the crowd into an even louder frenzy!

I couldn't help but feel like I'd already lost when he played that second beat. But this wasn't a time to retreat or think negatively about the situation, so I kept reminding myself that this was ALL OR NOTHING. The only thing I had left in my bag of tricks was a beat where I sampled the popular kid's cartoon, *Captain Planet*.

To my surprise the crowd got even louder than they did for his second beat, making me feel like I *might* have a slight chance of pulling off an upset.

But ultimately it wasn't up to the crowd. My fate was in the hands of the judges. After we played our last beats, the judges had a quick huddle and requested an overtime round. I was so shocked and excited that I almost forgot I had to play another beat. I looked like a contestant running down the aisle on *The Price Is Right* when their name's called to "COME ON DOOOOWN!"

I pulled myself together and looked over the list of beats I had left.

Not much.

I reminded myself again—ALL OR NOTHING—and picked the best beat I had left.

The beat I chose was another instrumental that sampled a TV show theme from *The Carol Burnett Show*. The response from the crowd was mediocre at best. I tried to enhance the reaction with some onstage antics, but it was too little too late. As my one-minute timer ran out I felt like I'd played the wrong beat.

Dibia$e's went in for the absolute kill. He played a beat that sampled the *Ghostbusters* theme song—and received the loudest reaction of the night, ensuring my humble return home with an "L" in my pocket.

I walked off the stage with mixed emotions. One part of me was disappointed because I'd felt so close to winning but didn't seal the deal. The other part of me was excited that I'd been able to get as far as I had.

Dibia$e went on to win the entire battle that night. I stayed until the end to congratulate him on a well-executed victory. He thanked me and expressed how I'd kept him on his toes during our battle. He also complimented my sampling skills and my overall progression since the last time we'd met.

Now I might have lost the battle that night, but those encouraging words from Dibia$e made me feel like a champion. I couldn't believe that somebody as legendary as him was again showering my music with that kind of respect. I was honored.

But the competitor in me still wanted another shot at him!

THE RED BULL BIG TUNE BEAT BATTLE

When Dibia$e first showed up on my radar I did extensive research on him. One of the first things that popped up on a YouTube search was an interview he did with the popular energy drink company, Red Bull. The interview was a profile piece for the contestants in the annual Red Bull Big Tune Beat Battle. There was no beat battle bigger than this one. Audiences showed up at it by the thousands to watch some of the country's best producers battle it out.

I desperately wanted to battle in this competition after watching Dibia$e's interview. I felt it could take me to another level of notoriety as a producer. When I finally got a chance to ask Dibia$e about it, he told me how it put him on lot of important people's radars and brought him new customers for his beats. At the time my beat sales were decent, but not enough to make a living from—maybe a few hundred dollars on a good month, which was quickly eaten up by my bills.

Not to mention that the money my grandfather had left us was quickly diminishing. It also didn't help that the rent in Rancho was on the rise. The reality of our situation was that if I didn't do something to help my mom with the finances soon we were going to lose our townhome.

In 2010, I had a few nonpaying placements with TDE, but I still didn't have an official major-label placement. I was getting a reputation but it wasn't being monetized. I needed to level up and create something on my own or receive an alley-oop to push me to that next level.

That alley-oop came in the form of a group email from none other than Dibia$e, addressed to Captain and me. Apparently, the higher-ups at Red Bull had put Dibia$e in charge of scouting young, talented producers to take part in the 2010 Red Bull Big Tune competition in Los Angeles. All Captain and I had to do was submit our three best beats and a high-resolution photo of ourselves.

I couldn't believe it. I responded to Dibia$e with a million thank-yous and attached the requested items. If all was approved, I would be getting the rare opportunity to compete in the biggest beat battle of my career.

A few weeks later Captain and I found out we'd been accepted. I sent a million prayers to the sky and jumped around my room like I was in a mosh pit with myself.

Captain and I received invitations to join legendary producer Jake One, the Red Bull staff, and our potential opponents for dinner in Los Angeles. Because Captain and I were the only ones coming from the Inland Empire we rode to the dinner together. The only thing we talked about the entire hour-long drive was what this battle meant for our careers—and, in a way, for the entire Inland Empire.

We knew we were the underdogs in the eyes of Los Angeles; we lived on the outskirts of the county. For many years the IE was viewed as "rustic" by LA—we were the weird country bumpkin cousins. Nevertheless, Captain and I went looking to represent the IE in the best light possible.

The Red Bull Big Tune dinner was held at a swanky restaurant in LA—gourmet burgers and a live piano player who took requests. When we first arrived, we had to sign in with the Red Bull staff and take a press photo for the competition. As I looked at the professional camera equipment they were using just to snap our photos, it set in just how big a deal this competition was.

> **As I looked at the professional camera equipment they were using just to snap our photos, it set in just how big a deal this competition was.**

We were led to a huge round table to sit with the other competitors. The table was decked out with wine and glass bowls filled with ice and Red Bull energy drinks. The first few minutes were awkwardly silent. I assumed it was because every producer there was nervous about the competition being only a few days away. Or perhaps this was another case of producers naturally being weirdos when removed from their natural habitat.

The ice was broken when one of the producers directed a question to the entire table: what does everyone use to make their beats?

Counterclockwise around the table you heard the same kinds of answers: Reason, Logic, and MPCs. These answers stayed pretty consistent until the question made its way to our side of the table and it was Captain's turn to answer. We both looked at each other and answered in unison: "FruityLoops."

The table once again fell awkwardly silent. Friendly smiles turned into frowns of disapproval. Even the original questioner snickered to himself in disapproval. In fact, he was so disgusted with our answer that it inspired him to deliver a bitter, three-minute rant about how FruityLoops is trash.

I was already pretty used to this response from older producers. Captain, on the other hand, was quietly boiling with anger. I don't think I've ever seen anybody grip a butter knife that tight; he probably could've squeezed butter back out of the knife. I knew he wanted to say something in response, but he wisely chose to smile instead. Captain was a no-nonsense type of guy, but he knew we were under the watchful eye of the Red Bull Big Tune staff. Especially since we were last-minute, special guests of Dibia$e.

On the long drive home Captain vowed to destroy that producer if he got the chance to battle him at Big Tune. I echoed those sentiments. There hadn't been any reason for the guy to attack us or the program we chose to create our music on. We both wanted to make him regret it.

WHAT'S IN THE MIX?

The battle was only a few days away and I prepared for it day and night. I searched every CD I'd ever used for a beat battle and grabbed the best beats I could find. The biggest critique from judges at past beat battles related to the mix on my beats. The truth of the matter was that I didn't know how to properly mix them. It wasn't until earlier that very year that I'd had access to a quality mix when I got signed to an IE-based record label called Black Cloud Music. Jynxx, the CEO and engineer of that label, taught me how to *properly* mix my beats.

I use the term "properly" very loosely, because as I pointed out earlier, there is no wrong or right way to mix a beat. However, there are some techniques agreed upon by most producers and engineers that can bring more clarity and space out of a beat. In my opinion, no matter how obsessed you are with communicating *your* sound, these techniques should never fall upon deaf ears. My general rule of thumb: try a new technique out and see how it makes you feel. If the end result of using the technique feels right, use it. If the end result doesn't feel right, don't use it. The point I want to drive home with you is that for long-term success as a producer you must understand the rules of mixing *before you break them* in the name of self-expression.

Jynxx understood this concept very well. He would approach every mix with a conscious balance of technique and creativity. When other engineers had tried to show me how to mix it sounded like they were trying to take the essence and soul out of my beats. It just didn't feel like

> *As a producer you must understand the rules of mixing before you break them in the name of self-expression.*

they understood my sound. They seemed to forget that Hip Hop makes its own rules; our music lives in the *red* on the decibel meter.

Jynxx understood exactly what I was trying to accomplish. By the time he was showing me how to mix we'd already started to develop chemistry in the studio. He knew exactly how I wanted my beats to sound: loud, warm and clear.

So one night before the Red Bull Big Tune battle Jynxx helped me meticulously mix every single beat I wanted to play. He fully understood how big an opportunity this was for the IE, the label, and myself as a producer. As he mixed and EQ'd each sound, he showed me the significance of using a limiter and a parametric equalizer to give my beats room to breathe. I soaked it all up. By the end of our session I felt completely prepared for *war*.

THE DAY OF BIG TUNE

In the back of my mind I had an idea of how big this battle was going to be. But nothing could've prepared me for what I felt when I first walked inside the legendary LA venue where the battle was being held: the El Rey Theatre. The first thing I noticed was how far away the roof was from the ground. It looked like a theatre fit for a Shakespearean play.

Most of the producers were already there, spread throughout the empty venue and going through their own rituals in preparation for the battle. Before we knew it, the jumbotrons were fired up with our photos, the lights were shining bright, and the doors were officially open to the public.

Outside of Captain and Dibia$e I didn't talk much to the other competitors. I was nervous and didn't want them to know it. Instead I reminded myself I was there for a reason—and that I deserved to be there.

When the competition finally began the lights were blinding and the crowd was ready to hear some beats. In the first round Captain smashed right through his opponent. It was evident he was out for blood. He danced his way across the stage as his beats blasted loudly through the speakers.

His confidence gave *me* the confidence to move from behind the producer booth to dance. Now, mind you, Captain could *really* dance and I couldn't. My first attempts at interpretive dancing were extremely awkward, but I just kept going.

My hand was shaking uncontrollably that first round as I tried to work the DJ controls in front of the sold-out crowd. That nervousness was gone as soon as I heard the beginning of my beat blasting out of the humongous speakers. The first beat I played sampled sound effects from the popular video game *Street Fighter 2*. Each time a sound effect came on I acted it out in the direction of my opponent. This showmanship made the crowd go crazy. Each time the crowd screamed for me, I got just a little more juiced to keep dancing. Before I knew it, the judges were asking the crowd who they thought won the round.

I won by a landslide.

And then...

Host: Next round! Curtiss King versus DIBIA$E!!

My heart sank. I had to battle Dibia$e this early in the competition? As the returning LA champ, he was the obvious crowd favorite. He smashed right through his first round, and it was obvious he hadn't come to mess around. I was backstage looking at my handwritten list of beat titles, planning my attack. I remember propping myself up against a wall, eyes closed, trying to imagine myself winning the battle. As I completed my daydream I opened my eyes to see one of the most legendary West Coast producers of all time walk by.

I was star-struck. I thought to myself, *As if the stakes aren't already high enough, DJ Battlecat decides to just nonchalantly walk backstage.* Instantly all I could think about were the classics he'd produced for Snoop Dogg. But before I could fully process it I was called back onstage.

I played the best beats I had against Dibia$e. We went back and forth, trading jabs like seasoned UFC fighters. I used what I'd learned from our last battle and treated my second round against him like it was the final round of the competition. Dibia$e appeared unfazed by my attempts. He did just as I'd watched him do many battles before: listened calmly without much reaction, then stepped forward when it was his turn and played his classics.

In the end the crowd unanimously chose Dibia$e as the winner. I congratulated my brother with a handshake and wished him the best in the following rounds.

I went backstage with my head held high because I knew I'd given it my all. I'd simply lost to the better producer that night, not to mention to the same man responsible for getting me on that stage. I couldn't be mad at the results because I'd done what I was supposed to do.

Backstage I focused my attention on being Captain's ringside support. We congratulated each other like teammates because we were collectively making our presence felt. The IE came out in packs that night. Dozens upon dozens of our friends were in attendance hoping to cheer at least one of us on to victory. Captain was our last hope.

The next round something truly magical happened that only God could have scripted. Captain got exactly what he'd been wanting since that notorious Red Bull dinner days before. The host read off the names of a second-round matchup starring Captain and that bitter producer who'd been taking shots at FruityLoops.

To this day, I haven't seen one producer more hell bent on embarrassing another than Captain was that night. Beat by beat, Captain demolished this man—and the crowd let it be known. The other producer's fans tried their best to make the case for their guy, but Captain had too much sauce that night. That LA audience had never heard anything like Captain's beats or seen anything like his dancing in a beat battle. Thanks to a raucous reaction from the crowd, Captain advanced to the final round.

Before Captain walked off the stage the host announced that due to an odd number of producers being left in the battle, a special wildcard round was necessary. This meant that one of the producers who'd lost in the previous round could be voted back into the competition by the crowd. One of those producers eligible for the wildcard vote was me!

As I walked on I noticed my friends from the IE smiling and bubbling in anticipation of *screaming* me into the next round. As if this scenario couldn't be any more perfect, another one of the wildcard contestants was that bitter producer who'd just lost to Captain. The host asked the audience to make noise for their choice, and the reaction wasn't even close. The cheers from the IE section were so loud they nearly brought me to tears. The only reason I didn't cry was because of the hilarity of seeing that bitter producer take the walk of shame. He'd just been beat by two producers who used FruityLoops. I went from packing up for the night to frantically looking back at my list to see what I had left for my next opponent. It didn't even cross my mind who I was going to be competing against until the host announced:

"UH OH! Next round! Curtiss King versus DIBIA$E, part 2!!"

This time I wasn't nervous at all. I truly didn't give a damn about losing because it had already happened that night. My mentality was to no longer play defense against Dibia$e but to play *offense* on the audience. I had a second chance to make my mark because of my friends from the IE. Dibia$e was the crowd favorite, but I had enough support there to at least make the outcome interesting.

Dibia$e went first. He played a beat that combined a sample of a gospel choir with video game sound effects, and as expected the crowd lost their minds. By this time, I didn't even notice that DJ Battlecat was onstage listening to the battle because I was too focused on the task at hand. My first beat sampled a Marvin Gaye acapella and incorporated video game sound effects from a Game Boy game called *Metroid*. I called the beat "Metroid Marvin." Not

> *This time I wasn't nervous at all. I'd already lost once that night. Now I had a second chance to make my mark.*

only did the crowd go crazy for it, but DJ Battlecat started dancing to it onstage! Suddenly, what was once a competition in the palm of Dibia$e's hands slowly but surely started shifting in favor of the awkward kid from the IE.

Dibia$e sensed this shift and had the perfect beat to sway them back into his corner: that same *Ghostbusters* beat he'd smashed me with months ago at the Kill That Noise battle in the IE.

The crowd of over eight-hundred people went absolutely nuts. I kept my composure and didn't let their reaction phase me.

The last beat I played was created with a crowd's reaction in mind. I started the beat off purposely sounding minimal and amateurish—terrible synthetic drum sounds that made the whole thing seem like it lacked any potential. This horrible loop played out for about fifteen seconds, to where I'd added a long pause in the beat to make it seem like something had malfunctioned. Just as I'd planned, when the pause came up someone in the audience booed me . . . until an audio clip of Kanye West uttering the phrase, "I'm really happy for you, but I'ma let you finish" came on.

And then BOOM!!!! The REAL beat came on, and the crowd went ballistic.

Nobody that night came as close as I did to beating Dibia$e. After that round was complete all you heard were sounds of doubt from the crowd because there was no clear winner in our second duel. The battle could've easily gone either way. In fact, when the decision was left up to the crowd, Dibia$e and I both thought it was in my favor, but then the judges did a recount. I had already put my hands up, expecting to be handed the win and to move on to the final round against Captain.

The hosts, however, had other plans. They decided that the crowd reaction wasn't convincing enough in either direction, so we needed to take our battle to OT.

At that moment I started feeling like maybe the odds were stacked against me, like maybe the higher-ups thought I was out of line going at the golden child Dibia$e the way that I did. But in my mind this was a battle and I did what I was supposed to do—go for it and not hold back regardless of respect for my opponent.

I ended up losing that overtime match with Dibia$e fair and square. I made a terrible beat selection and Dibi won convincingly. I had literally run out of beats to play that night that could have matched up with his. I had to take full responsibility for that loss. Thankfully, I didn't leave that stage feeling like a loser. I walked off smiling.

As I wandered backstage to find Captain and cheer him on, DJ Battlecat walked up to me and said, "Job well done tonight, young man." All I could do was smile and say thank you.

When I finally found Captain he too congratulated me on a hard-fought battle. We talked about what the possible ripple effect might be for our careers because of our performances that night. Would it mean more placements? Would it mean more beat sales? We didn't know. All we knew for sure was that Captain had already secured a ticket to Chicago regardless of whether he beat Dibia$e in the last round or not.

And as it turned out, Dibia$e went on to win that battle. In retrospect, I feel that was the way God intended it to happen. In the final round, Captain had already got the win he wanted versus that other producer, so he wasn't interested in beating Dibia$e. To end the night, both competitors played non-confrontational beats against each other, and Dibia$e took home the victory.

Dibia$e accepted his first-place trophy and I congratulated him and thanked him again for the opportunity. As he had done many times before, he showered me with respect and admiration for the work I'd done that night.[10]

As I walked through the crowd looking for my friends, stranger after stranger showed me love. Some people asked to take pictures with the man who'd taken the legendary Dibia$e to overtime. I was overwhelmed, and I felt proud of myself in a way I'd never done before.

The very next day I edited the footage one of my Black Cloud Music labelmates, Yasin, had captured on a digital camera. As I chopped and replayed each clip I got goosebumps. It felt like I was reliving the night. When the videos were finished rendering I put them on a DVD so I could show my mom when she got off work.

Scan the QR Code to watch the 2010 Red Bull Big Tune Beat Battle.

By the end of that video my mom was in tears. She said, "All

---

[10] Captain & Curtiss King at Red Bull Big Tune: https://www.youtube.com/watch?v=WtbxEenQwj0

those people are screaming for my son? Oh, my gosh."

It didn't matter to her that I'd lost to Dibia$e, because in her eyes I was already a winner for fearlessly pursuing my dreams. She was so proud of her son for competing and doing it his own way. Her reaction put the biggest smile on my face. It was one thing to make my peers proud of me, but to make my mom so proud that she cried? That feeling was unforgettable.

The next few weeks the social media conversations about a producer named Curtiss King increased dramatically. Although Red Bull Big Tune didn't necessarily bring me more rappers that wanted to buy my beats, it definitely made more producers fans of my work. This was a big opportunity. There had to be a way I could capitalize on this newfound notoriety and keep the flames roaring.

But how?

TV THEMES FLIPPED MIXTAPE

The answer came to me late one night on Twitter while chopping it up with one of my producer homies, Jansport J.

It started off as a simple #TVThemesFlipped Twitter hashtag and a challenge between Jansport J and myself: create a beat from scratch that sampled one of our favorite TV themes. About an hour later our hashtag challenge started to go viral in the producer community. Before we knew it, producers started to upload new beats using our hashtag. About two hours later over thirty producers had

> *While I was busy ripping and running through beat battles and producing for Ab-Soul albums, trying to make a name for myself, there were kids who had literally grown up watching me do it.*

contributed new beats and tweets to join in on the challenge. Most of the beats the producers were submitting under that hashtag were fire. That's when I decided to hop on the phone with Jansport J and run the idea of turning the hashtag challenge into an impromptu project. He was down with it because most of the work was already done. When we got off the phone, I made an announcement on Twitter that I was going to compile beats from the hashtag to form a spontaneous project. When I made that announcement, I got a random tweet from a graphic designer asking to create the cover for us. The next morning, I found myself uploading the cover art and top beats from the hashtag challenge onto my Bandcamp.

TV Themes Flipped Volume 1 was born.

The most important thing I learned from that experience was that a lot of producers looked up to me. They saw me as a leader in the producer community. Apparently, I was the last one to notice it, but that hashtag challenge experience opened my eyes.

While I was busy ripping and running through beat battles and producing for Ab-Soul albums, trying to make a name for myself, there were kids who had literally grown up watching me do it. Each time I took the legendary Dibia$e to overtime, these kids were following my every move.

When I finally realized how many of my peers looked up to me I tried my best to lead by example. Knowing that I had other producers watching my every move both empowered and frightened me.

In *my* eyes, I was still an up-and-coming producer without a major-label placement.

In *my* eyes, I wasn't jack until I could start making money off my music.

In *their* eyes, I was already *something*.

Lessons to Take Away from Chapter 10

1. Mixing is the translation of your musical ideas to your audience.
2. There is no wrong or right way to mix when it represents the sounds within you.
3. Try different mixing techniques and gauge how they make you feel in spite of their popularity.
4. Beat battles can put your name on the map as a producer.
5. In life you will either willingly become humble or get humbled.
6. As Les Brown would say, the fight isn't over until you win!
7. Seize the opportunities that come your way and give everything you've got.
8. It's not about what you use as producer, but how you use it.
9. If you are shy, put yourself in situations that will force you to come out of your shell.
10. Real legends pay it forward.

CHAPTER 11

PLAY
THE BEAT

*"When I think about placements I try to put myself in the
mindset of what the artist needs."*

~ Seige (Producer)

So, the beat is complete, what now? I'd say it's time to get
another creative partner involved! That involvement could
come in the form of constructive feedback from a friend and/or
possibly a rapper who can use words to further tell the story of your
beat. If I had to choose a direction to go in first, I would probably
choose to get a rapper involved before I asked for feedback from a
non-musician friend. I made this very common mistake early on when
asking my music listener friends—who had never crafted a beat in
their lives—for their technical opinion about my music. I wasn't
interested in hearing how the beat made them *feel*; I wanted to hear
their thoughts on how I could improve my kick and snare mixes.

Not a smart move. To my credit, I wanted to see if they believed my beats were good enough to get placed or purchased. The only problem with their feedback was that they weren't the ones purchasing my beats! Don't get me wrong; I knew there was some value in their feedback, but what I really needed to do was get my work in front of the decision makers and potential buyers—aka the rappers.

Rappers get a lot of flak from music producers for being difficult people to work with, but at the end of the day we need each other. When a rapper and producer are on the same page there is no denying the cohesive chemistry of their music. I know this because I've been on both sides of the recording booth. I know from producing Keyden the importance of hearing his feedback on the difficulties my beats presented him when writing songs. I know from working with John when *I* was the rapper that as a producer he saw the bigger picture and helped me become more efficient in the studio. Most importantly, I know the value of getting your music around elite creative energies. In my case, when I worked with TDE it caused me to elevate my game and play ball on a whole new level.

Initially, my pursuit of a major placement also provided me a much-needed boost of creative elevation.

> *Most producers I know grew up dreaming about the day they'd get their first major-label placement. I was no different.*

Most producers I know grew up dreaming about the day they'd get their first major-label placement. I was no different. Just the thought of seeing my name on the credits for an official major-label album, movie soundtrack, or television commercial gave me goosebumps. Even in the beginning of my career, it drove me to do my best to compete with the elite music producers in my industry.

The thought that music I'd created in an apartment or on a patio could end up on an album with production credits like Alchemist and 9th Wonder lit a fire under me. The idea that music I'd made in a home studio all by myself could end up being performed in front of hundreds of thousands of screaming fans—and that I'd get *paid* for it—kept me working late into the night.

When I discuss the topic of placements in my career, most people immediately refer to my work with Ab-Soul. But in my eyes, a placement was never quite a placement unless I received a check made out with my government name for it. With that said, my first paid placement came from a very unorthodox and unexpected source.

VANS DOWNTOWN SHOWDOWN

Rewind back to 2009. Before I'd made my official move to the IE, a friend of mine in Carson named Robbin invited me to a skateboard competition at Paramount Studios. Robbin worked for a video production company called Window Seat Entertainment. Window Seat oversaw the video highlights for an annual VANS event called the VANS Downtown Showdown.

VANS, an apparel company, would take over the Paramount Studios movie lot and host skateboard competitions. Professional skateboarders from all over the U.S. competed in various competitions in front of a live studio audience. I was never a skateboarder myself, but I was a huge fan of the skateboard culture thanks to my introduction to it via Tony Hawk's skateboard video game franchise on PlayStation.

I didn't go to the event expecting to get a placement with VANS, but Robbin was really and truly looking out for me that night. She instructed me to bring a CD of my beats, just in case a networking opportunity arose. Then as soon as I got to the venue I was ushered by Robbin directly into the backstage area to meet the staff at Window

Seat Entertainment.

This was the first time I'd ever been behind the scenes for something that elaborate. As spectators at big events we often don't realize the number of people and the amount of work needed to pull them off. While everyone on the outside was busy eating corn dogs and watching their favorite skateboarders perform tricks, behind the scenes dozens of people were chugging coffee and energy drinks, working around the clock to cover it all.

Robbin introduced me to everyone as an accomplished music producer. It was the first time I'd ever heard anyone describe me that way. In my eyes I'd just worked on a few records with homies who were doing well. Now with every introduction she made it dawned on me that my credits *meant* something. Because of Robbin I started to look at my production credits as legitimate marks on my music résumé.

One of the people Robbin introduced me to was the CEO of the video company—one of the coolest CEOs I've ever met. He was young, laid back, and very chill with his staff, the opposite of the uptight suit-and-tie CEO I expected him to be. He was dressed comfortably head-to-toe in VANS apparel and slippers, which made him look more like he was on his way to the beach. We only spoke briefly, but he treated me with the utmost respect. I thought to myself, *Now this is the type of entrepreneur I hope to be someday.*

Before we parted the CEO mentioned that his company was searching for background music for the video highlights his company was compiling for VANS. They were more than willing to pay for that music. I handed him my CD of beats and gave him my email.

I was excited and extremely thankful, but I knew better than to let my expectations get too high. After all, I'd been down this road before when I'd handed Ab a CD of my beats and heard nothing back until a year later. Still, as I watched the skateboarders compete I couldn't help but imagine what they'd look like skating with my beats in the background . . .

A month later I heard back from Robbin's company via an email that said:

Window Seat Entertainment: Hey Curtiss! We just wanted to inform you that we chose 3 instrumentals from your CD that we thought would fit perfectly in our video highlights! We are prepared to pay you $200 for your work. Please contact us at your earliest convenience.

I read that email back about ten times in disbelief. I don't know if I was more excited that three of my beats were chosen or that I'd be getting paid for my work. Either way I didn't waste any time responding to them with the information they wanted. Within a few minutes I received another email.

Window Seat Entertainment: Ok awesome! Thanks for getting back so fast! Oh, also please provide us your ASCAP or BMI information. Thanks!

ASCAP OR BMI?

Oh, crap.

Those words terrified me. In fact, almost ALL music business terminology was terrifying to me back then. It wasn't because I was too lazy to look it up, but because I was afraid of getting the wrong information. At this point I didn't have any mentors I could ask about this kind of thing so I had to put my trust in the Internet. I was vaguely familiar with the companies ASCAP and BMI, but I wasn't 100% sure what their purpose was.

I did some quick research and pulled information from multiple sources. ASCAP and BMI are Performing Rights Organizations in charge of seeking out royalties on behalf of musicians when their music is used. It's like having a union at a job. Members get to enjoy the security of having an organization with their back financially. In my brief research, I saw more positive things said about ASCAP, so given the time constraints I chose to sign with them.

> **ASCAP and BMI are Performing Rights Organizations in charge of seeking out royalties on behalf of musicians when their music is used. It's like having a union at a job. Members get to enjoy the security of having an organization with their back financially.**

Thankfully the process was a lot faster at that time than it is now. (If this is something you haven't looked into yet, I suggest researching your options now.) I submitted my application and notified the video company that I was waiting to receive my member number. About two days later I got it.

Three weeks later I received a package in the mail from VANS. I unwrapped it like a child on Christmas Day. Inside was a pink thank-you note, a check for $200, and a DVD entitled *2009 VANS Downtown Showdown*. The DVD was only about fifteen minutes long—but it felt like an eternity as I waited to see the scenes with my beats behind them.

The video was amazing, including highlights and interviews with the skateboarders at the event. I watched and waited patiently until out of nowhere my beat blasted through while Alex Olson, Raven Tershay, Rick McCrank, Andrew Langi, Vincent Alvarez and Jani Laitiala did skateboard tricks.

The combination of joy, goosebumps, and pride I felt while watching was overwhelming. I texted Robbin soon after and thanked her again for the opportunity.

MY FIRST VIDEO GAME PLACEMENT: *APB: RELOADED*

In the music industry, your success will ultimately be contingent upon who you know. I'm sure you've heard that said a million and one times, but it's the absolute truth.

But . . . The thing is that most times we think that "who" has to be someone famous. That's not the case, and I've also learned from experience that the individual in question isn't always someone you expect it to be.

Case in point: my friend and mentor, Komboa.

Komboa was an accomplished, multilingual emcee and spectacular graphic designer who consistently collaborated with my label, Black Cloud Music. He was responsible for the artwork on my debut album, *Atychiphobia*. Komboa has always been a straight shooter with a kind heart. When he says he's going to do something, you'd better believe he will.

One morning in 2011, Komboa called me to discuss a possible placement opportunity at his job. Komboa worked for a company called Ayzenberg. This was an ad agency that created media campaigns for movies and video games. They needed energetic music for an online adventure game they were working on: *APB: Reloaded*. Komboa mentioned my name and they took me on. I'd be spending nine hours a day creating that music. I was beyond excited.

The office was a forty-five-mile commute away. Unfortunately, at that time my car had been repossessed—more on that later—but Komboa offered to take me with him to work.

He introduced me to everyone at Ayzenberg, including his boss, Jon. Although the work sounded fun, the employees and environment were serious and professional. Every office was equipped with a state-of-the art computer that must have been expensive as hell.

I stuck out like a sore thumb for two reasons: I had a blonde flattop and carried a laptop that my friends had nicknamed "Frankenstein."

Frankenstein was a broken, seventeen-inch, navy-blue Dell computer with a loose neck. Where most laptops are supposed to smoothly bend, Frankenstein unapologetically gave out. Years of me packing it into undersized backpacks eventually broke it.

A couple of years before I'd opened it one night after a show and the screen snapped back so far that the power button came off. I had to swing the screen back and forth until it turned back on. This took anywhere from ten minutes to two hours. Once it finally booted up, I had to keep it on for days just to avoid having to do it all over again.

> **I stuck out like a sore thumb for two reasons: I had a blonde flattop and a broken laptop my friends had nicknamed "Frankenstein."**

Thankfully, as a Hip Hop producer I didn't worry much about my peers making fun of me and that laptop. At this juncture in Hip Hop, we had a habit of viewing the *struggle* as a sign of authenticity. As producers, we were creating music in basements, on patios, and in home studios, so it was okay I was THAT guy. Even when I went to professional studios I could always find a dark corner in which to resuscitate Frankenstein.

But now, as the center of attention in the Ayzenberg office, there wasn't much chance of finding any dark corners to hide in. In fact, Jon set me up at a very well-lit computer desk next to his office and directly in front of the video game designers. As I set my station up I said a silent prayer for Frankenstein to turn on without any problems.

Dear God, please allow Frankenstein to act right this morning. This opportunity is too important. It's paying and I'm broke. Too broke for Frankenstein to get in the way of me working today. Please allow him to work. PLEASE!

Amen.

That morning God reminded me of his sense of humor. It took me almost twenty-five, real-life, adult minutes to get that computer to turn on. In the background I overheard whispers and silent giggles from the video game designers as I swung the neck of my laptop back and forth. I wasn't trying to make a scene, but that didn't stop me from making a scene.

Jon came out a few times to check if I was ready for his instructions, saw the struggle was real, and returned to his office. Eventually Frankenstein came to life and I went to tell Jon.

His office was a video gamer's paradise: flat screen monitors, surround-sound speakers, popular video game action figures in a glass case, a comfortable leather chair, and classic video game posters framed on every wall.

Jon gave me a preview of the project's trailer with its original, uncleared music. He spoke nonchalantly about the CGI graphics used in the commercial and how it was nowhere close to a finished product quite yet—but I thought it looked incredible. The more he talked about all the work that had gone into the trailer, the more I felt the pressure. It was like my studio session with Ghrimm and Ab-Soul all over again. I honestly started to doubt whether or not I could deliver what they needed musically. Weren't there a thousand other producers more qualified than me to do this job?

In fact, I had about ten producers on my cell phone alone who would've killed for the opportunity. Some producers I know ONLY look for opportunities to work with companies like this and don't even bother pursuing major-label placements with major-label artists. They know there's a difference between working with rappers and working with corporations. Corporations usually pay more and faster, minus all of the unnecessary politics of the music industry.

When it comes to pursuing placements with major-label artists, the politics are flat-out outrageous in comparison. There is so much red tape, time, and doubt that passes between the moments your music is actually accepted, placed, and paid for.

But more on that later.

Jon gave me a copy of the trailer and a list of sounds, moods, and cue points he needed me to tackle. He wasn't a music producer himself, so he struggled a bit with the terminology, but I got a good grasp on what he was looking for. The commercial needed a beat that was dark, edgy, and energetic. I sat at my desk skimming through a few beats I'd compiled the night before to see if anything matched his description.

> *Corporations usually pay more and faster. When it comes to placements with major-label artists, a lot of red tape, time, and doubt pass between the moments your music is accepted, placed, and paid for.*

There were probably about three out of the thirty beats I had that really fit. I think Jon was expecting me to just bring him the music but I decided to go a step beyond that. After all, I didn't learn video-editing for nothing, right? I spent about ten minutes matching the video to my beats and exporting the drafts, then walked back into Jon's office to show him the final product.

He was impressed. He appreciated the fact that I'd taken the initiative to match the video to my beats and provide him with multiple drafts. I sat down, hoping to see an immediate positive reaction as he cycled through the three videos. Instead Jon played one of the videos three times straight, paused thoughtfully, then looked me in the eyes and said, "Yes, Curtiss this is the one."

I gave a huge sigh of relief. But I wasn't finished for the day—not hardly. Jon made a list of about twenty changes he wanted for the next draft. I accepted every instruction and asked thorough questions to clarify exactly what he wanted done, then took the list back to my desk to make the changes.

We repeated this process for the next seven hours. As I made new changes to the music, Jon requested changes to the changes. As I worked he watched the video on loop looking for more ways to enhance the changes he'd requested on the original changes. Every five minutes he would return to my desk with another idea he wanted me to try out. The more excited he got, the more change crazy he became, but I was up for the challenge. I could tell he was happy to have me in the Ayzenberg building; I was the first music producer they'd ever had work onsite.

By 5:00 p.m., I gave him what I thought would be the final draft. Once again, I was wrong. He asked me to come in one more day to finalize the project.

So the next day I drove in again with Komboa, and along the way we talked about more than just music. We talked about life and what it meant to be a man. It was the first time I felt I was speaking to someone older and wiser than me who understood my world as a musician and how I could balance it with my personal life. He too had been a Hip Hop artist—a very successful one internationally. He also had a family he loved dearly and would give everything to take care of. My girl at the time had a son, so seeing him talk about the example he tried to set for his own son resonated deeply with me as a stepdad.

I mention all this because after our talks it was evident to me that I had a lot of growing up to do. I had to question whether my music could provide for my family.

On day two at Ayzenberg, Jon gave me the good news that East Coast rapper Chaundon had recorded a verse to my beat that would be included in the commercial. I was already familiar with Chaundon at that time so I was excited about adding him to my production credits.

By the end of the day the commercial score was done and I was thanked repeatedly for my involvement. The drive home was bittersweet. I was already missing the feeling of waking up every day and going to a job that required me to simply make music for a living. I was also going to miss my motivational talks with Komboa. He dropped a lot of gems on me during those commutes, and before he dropped me off at home that night he blessed me with one I'll never forget:

Komboa: Know your worth, or one day someone will determine it for you.

I listened to his words and never let them leave my side.

MY FIRST MAJOR PLACEMENT DURING THE GREAT RECESSION

I loved living in the city of Rancho Cucamonga with my mom and sisters. It was one of the happiest times of my twenties. For the first time, we all experienced what it was like not to *worry* about money. That townhome was our paradise, and thanks to what we had left over from my mom selling my grandparents' house we had some much-needed breathing room.

Unfortunately our taste of paradise would soon turn sour.

From 2007 until about 2009 the talk on every news station was about the Great Recession. It would go down in history as the largest economic downturn since the Great Depression. The unemployment rate was higher than what most of us had experienced in our lifetimes. And although the history books say it only lasted for two years, I will always remember a crippling ripple effect that lasted much longer.

After our first year in Rancho, the money my mom had saved from selling the house was starting to run out. My oldest sister Jazmine was having issues in college and needed to move back home. Word-of-mouth about my talents as a rapper and producer were at an all-time high, but the harsh reality was that I was flat broke. Soon my mom started to put pressure on my oldest sister and me to look for jobs, and she had to return to work herself.

We all got hit hard financially. It was depressing to wake up and realize it might be one of the last times you'd do so in your own room. Eventually, we had to start receiving government assistance.

I wasn't selling many beats, and even when I did the money went towards the rent or my car note (on which I was already months behind). My relationship with my dad was still very rocky. My pride wouldn't allow me to ask him for help. I still had a burning desire to prove to him that I could accomplish my goals through my pursuit of music. I searched far and wide for a part-time job in the surrounding cities. I even signed up for a temporary work agency and applied for another sandwich restaurant job. But like most people that year, I couldn't find work.

I tried to convince myself that this was the part of my life story when a miracle would come sweeping through and set us free, that I was just one placement away from changing our situation for the better.

Then, one Sunday morning on Twitter I saw a message from an A&R named Ace Pun that read:

PRODUCERS! @Gmalone & @OfficialMack10 are looking for beats for their new album. Send 3 Heaters To this Email . . .

I thought to myself, *This must be the sign I'm looking for.*

At least, I wanted it to be a sign *so badly*. I didn't waste any time sending three of my best beats to Pun. Mack 10 was a West Coast legend and Glasses Malone was one of the biggest rappers around at that time. A placement on their collaborative album would not only be an amazing achievement but also an opportunity to get a placement check.

I've been told by my fellow producers that the first album placement is always the most difficult one to get. But once you get it your value increases in the industry, opening the floodgates for more placements. Rappers check out other rappers' albums, so placements land you on other people's radars and increase your visibility—leading to other placements.

Of course, I didn't know what to expect when I sent those beats out. For all I knew they'd be stolen and remade by another producer. But I was just desperate enough to take a chance on it.

After I hit send on that email, I did something my mom had been begging me to do for years: go to church. My mom knew I was working hard to make something big happen on my end, but she reminded me countless times that I couldn't do it without God. I'd prayed about our situation, but I still felt like something was missing; I thought maybe it was church.

The service was amazing that morning. The pastor spoke about the importance of taking chances when the odds are against us. I took that message to heart and thought about it all the way home. When I checked my email I saw a message from Ace Pun:

Ace Pun: Curtiss King, Glasses wants to use one of your beats for his album with Mack. Let me know if you're free tomorrow to come out to Long Beach and track it out.

Have you ever watched that final scene of the movie *Pursuit of Happyness*, when Will Smith's character does that celebratory fist pump with tears slowly rolling down his eyes? I felt the same exact way as I read that email. Glasses Malone and Mack 10 were releasing their collaborative album on Hoo-Bangin' Records, which was under the umbrella of Lil Wayne's label, Cash Money Records. This was set to be my first official major-label album placement. I say "official," because although most people assume my first major placements were with TDE, I never truly saw them as being placements because I wasn't paid for my work. However, with huge, major-label artists and labels being involved in my placement with Mack 10, I expected the pay to be bigger than anything I'd ever received.

Then, in the midst of this excitement, a sobering question crossed my mind.

How am I going to make it to Long Beach when I just spent my last few dollars on gas going to church?

I couldn't ask my mom for help because she needed every dollar she had to commute back and forth to work. I couldn't ask any of my friends because they weren't doing much better than I was. Additionally, I had too much pride to ask anybody else for help because, after all, Curtiss King was supposed to be doing well for himself.

I'd learned early on that in the music industry, image is key, so I felt like I couldn't tell Pun I was too broke to make the drive. I ended up lying and saying I was having car troubles and couldn't make it that day; he responded telling me to keep him posted.

I felt like an idiot. Here was the biggest placement of my career and I couldn't even afford the gas to see it through.

MY FIRST MANAGER: STREET GODDESS

I didn't end up making it to that session with Ace Pun and Glasses Malone. I ended up sending the beat and its musical stems via email to their studio in Long Beach. I was disappointed in myself, but I wasn't defeated. After all, I was *still* going to get paid soon, right?

Not quite.

One thing I learned about placements from this experience is that they take time to process. It's often a long waiting game. A producer might get the good news that his beat has been placed on a major-label album but not see a check from it for a year.

In rare cases, some independent labels pay producers upfront fees. But that's not how my first paid placement panned out. I wasn't anybody special at the time and I had to wait—regardless of what I was going through financially.

I *did* have a little bit of luck in that I had recently hired a manager named Street Goddess who had a really good relationship with Glasses Malone and Pun.

I met Street Goddess when she did PR work for Top Dawg Entertainment in their early days. She was always looking out for me and would give me a heads-up when Kendrick or Jay Rock started working on new albums. When she decided to part ways with TDE and run her own PR company I asked her if she would be willing to help promote one of my albums. She knew I didn't have a lot of money but we agreed upon a discounted amount—$450—that I would pay her after I received my first placement check.

> *Placements can take time to process. It's often a long waiting game. A producer might get the good news that his beat has been placed on a major-label album but not see a check from it for a year.*

Producers, never make plans with money you don't currently have in your hand. I learned that the hard way when I made that agreement. The PR work Street Goddess did was well worth the money, but it was a financial risk that ended up biting me in the ass. My logic was that getting her to do PR work for my album would lead to more paid shows and placements. I took a risk in this situation: I let money and the allure of possible opportunity influence my decision making. I *assumed* $450 would only be a small fraction of the money that my major-label placement was going to pay me. That was a mistake.

I was so worried about ruining my working relationship with Pun that I didn't ask him how much I was going to get paid for the placement. In retrospect, I should've found a tactful way to ask, because I had a lot on the line. I just didn't want to appear desperate.

PURSUING MY DREAMS?

Meanwhile, back at home, the bills kept coming and our debt grew deeper. Our Internet was turned off after we were a few cycles late paying for it, so in order to send beats or check emails I had to steal Internet from a local Starbucks parking lot. I felt like a complete and utter loser.

Even worse, I started to feel like I'd been selfish for many years. I'd been pursuing *my* dreams and not taking anybody else's feelings into consideration. I thought about all the shows my mom had given me gas money to attend. I thought about the roof over my head that we were close to losing. I thought about the lack of food we had in the refrigerator, about the car I had in the parking lot that would probably be repossessed soon, and about all the possessions my mom had used her hard-earned dollars to pay for—and I came to the realization that we were about to lose it all.

> **Never make plans with money you don't have in your hand.**

I couldn't help but feel it was all my fault. How dare I fix my lips to call myself the "man" of the house? How could I let this happen to the women I loved the most in my life? How? Was this what I called "DOING IT FOR THE FAM"?!

I had thoughts of ending my life many times because of how worthless I felt. The main thing that stopped me was the thought that a funeral would merely be another expense my family couldn't afford.

Most days I felt like an expensive waste of air.

My mom, sensing this, reminded me to stay faithful and positive. In her eyes this was all only a test, and things would turn around soon. I did my best to believe her, but the voices in my head were much louder.

PLACEMENT CHECK

A few weeks later I finally caught a break. I got a call that my placement check was ready to be picked up from Long Beach. This time I scraped together change, and after a trip to Coinstar I put $15 in my tank and went to Glasses Malone's studio in Long Beach.

Glasses was at the front desk signing paperwork and I took a second to introduce myself to him. G shook my hand and thanked me for being a part of his album. In return I thanked him and Pun for allowing me to produce for the album. He seemed preoccupied with his paperwork and I didn't want to waste any more of his time so I kept the small talk brief. He gave me an envelope with my check in it and I left. I was so excited that I didn't even open the envelope to see how much I was getting paid. I just drove to the nearest check-cashing store . . . where I was in for an unpleasant surprise.

Check Cashing Cashier: Mr. Howard, do you have a DBA card that can show me proof you're doing business as Curtiss King?

The cashier handed back my check. To my disappointment, it was only for $500 *and* it was addressed to "Curtiss King" and not to my government name.

I got on the phone with Pun to let him know about the name situation. He promised he'd look into it but couldn't until the next work week when everybody was back in the Hoo-Bangin' offices. I drove home that night feeling even more defeated than before.

I came to understand that $500 wasn't bad for a first-time placement check. The only problem was that I owed my manager

$450 of it. The $50 that remained wasn't even going to put a dent in our past-due rent.

I thought about letting Street Goddess know about my situation, but she was counting on that money because she had a baby on the way. In fact, she was making daily phone calls to check on the status of our money.

By the time I got the revised check in the mail and paid Street Goddess, my family and I were packing up boxes to move. We had officially been evicted from our townhome oasis.

GOODBYE RANCHO CUCAMONGA, HELLO SAN BERNARDINO

No matter how many times you go through the process, you never quite get used to evictions. The first eviction I experienced was in 2001, when my mom and I got evicted from our apartment. It was a few days before Christmas and the Sheriff and complex manager stood outside smiling and waiting for us to get the last of our belongings. I was an angry eighteen-year-old looking at everything we owned spread out on the sidewalk. And even

> *If I was going to continue pursuing a career in music, it had to be on my own dime.*

though I wasn't a violent human being, I wanted desperately for somebody that day to say the wrong thing so I could take out all of my anger on something. I still have visions of that property owner smiling as all our clothes, dishes, photo albums, televisions, and blankets were stacked on the ground.

Fast forward to 2010, and here we were in much the same position. My mom had an opportunity to rent a room from a family friend in Compton and I was welcome to go with her. But I refused to be a burden to her anymore. I was too old to be acting so young. And if I was going to continue pursuing a career in music, it had to be on my own dime.

These were my dreams, not my mom's, and I had to stop being so selfish about them.

A few days before we officially moved I reached out to Jynxx and Yasin, my Black Cloud labelmates, to ask if I could stay with them until I got back on my feet. They agreed, and a few days later I drove to their apartment with a car full of everything I owned. I was thankful that they allowed me to stay in their apartment but I was honestly up to my neck in depression.

I wasn't the only one. We all had stories to tell. Those first few months were hell. All three of us were struggling financially. Jynxx was the only one who had a 9-5. Yasin and I had to figure out our own hustles to make ends meet. The only one I knew was my beats, so that's all I worked on day and night in the apartment. One of the first ideas I came up with was to drop a beat tape and put it up for sale. *Slum Beautiful* only sold ten copies.

The next idea I had was to sell my beats for ridiculously low prices to my email customers. I had an email list I'd developed over the years called the "Dish List." This was a list of customers who had purchased beats from me in the past. Every week I'd send out an email with the newest beats I had for sale. I only sold my beats for exclusive rights, meaning no other artists could rap over them except the buyer. Occasionally, I'd get requests from customers to make custom beats for a little more, but most of my customers wanted beats from the Dish List. I tried to use all the marketing and sales lessons I'd learned from Professor Morgan years before, but I was only able to hustle up about $80 a month.

That $80 had to somehow pay for my Internet bill, food, and essential hygiene products. I would have added gas to that list of expenses but Nissan had finally repossessed my car. Unfortunately, I lost everything in that repossession—from my high-school diploma to my marketing certificate to my grandpa's vinyls and even my irreplaceable photo albums. Because our apartment didn't have much room I had stupidly left these things in the car. I wasn't able to get my stuff from the dealership because I couldn't afford the fee to get it out of their storage.

Jynxx was really cool and understanding about my situation. He knew I wasn't going to be able to pay rent for the first few months. Plus, he knew I could provide Black Cloud Music value in many other ways. I could edit YouTube videos for our channel, design album covers for my labelmates, and make beats nonstop. It was a lot of work but I didn't mind doing it for three main reasons: I loved working, I had a place to stay, and working kept my mind off my growling stomach.

MAKING ENDS MEET

I have always loved food.

Food fills me with so much joy. Today the Food Channel is saved as one of my favorites on my cable box. One of my ex-girlfriends used to joke that anytime I got angry I was merely a Taco Bell chalupa away from being happy again.

The worst part about poverty at that time wasn't just the lack of money in my pockets. After all, some of my most amazing nights out with friends required little to no money to be spent. The worst part about poverty was looking at my meal and not knowing when the next one was coming. I had to eat with caution because my appetite was much bigger than my pockets could afford. We spent many nights in that apartment sharing $10 boxes of tacos and burritos from Del Taco which, by a

> *The worst part about poverty was looking at my meal and not knowing when the next one was coming.*

stroke of luck, was walking distance from our apartment.

However, we had to be very careful about when we went to get our food because Jynxx's landlord kept a watchful eye. Technically Jynxx was supposed to be the only one in that apartment, but of course there were three of us.

Speaking of the landlord, she was something else. Yasin was convinced she smoked meth religiously. I just thought she was nosey as hell, but I didn't think of her as having a drug habit. What she did have was a habit of appearing at random times and trying to catch us sleeping or using one of our personal keys to get inside the gate.

One time Jynxx caught her pointing a telescope in the direction of our apartment when he was smoking a cigarette on the balcony. I don't know how, but Yasin smooth-talked her into believing that we were merely hired to stay at Jynxx's apartment during the daytime to protect his studio equipment from crackheads. This wasn't a farfetched story to anyone living in that part of town.

San Bernardino is not a city for the weak. When we lived there, SB County was on the verge of filing for bankruptcy because they were over a billion dollars in debt. In addition, an article I read once said that SB's murder rate surpassed Chicago's between 2010 and 2016.

So it was a rough city to live in, but I spent most of my time there with my butt planted in my computer chair working on beats. Ironically, I think I was more scared of starving than I was of the city's murder rate. I wasn't eating right, and I surely wasn't eating enough. Everyone who brags about surviving poverty always champions the benefits of cheap meals like ramen noodles. I take a much different stance. I refuse to champion store-bought ramen noodles. During this period, I was binge-eating so many bags of ramen noodles that the high sodium gave me serious digestive issues. I also started getting intense migraines. Both issues could put me out of commission for days at time; that was extremely bad for business.

To be honest, I'm a little reluctant to share these stories; this is the first time I'm doing so. I don't want any of you to get the idea I'm bragging about having it rough. I don't wear my poverty as a badge of honor. In fact, I wasn't proud of my situation in the least bit. I was angry at myself for being too intelligent and talented to have landed in that mess.

I'm sharing these stories because even my heroes haven't told me all of *their* ugly truths. I think it's important to know that there was nothing glamorous or triumphant about those times, and that even the "smart" ones like you and me do stupid things and make stupid decisions. This is another possible reality of the journey through the industry. So as I get into this next story my hope is that it encourages you should you ever find yourself in a similar situation.

> *I don't wear my poverty as a badge of honor. I wasn't proud of my situation. I was angry at myself for being too intelligent and talented to have landed in that mess. But the ugly truth is that even the "smart" ones like you and me do stupid things and make stupid decisions. This is another possible reality of the journey through the industry.*

MY LOWEST OF LOWS

I spent a lot of alone time in that apartment. I worked tirelessly to try to flip my situation. I muscled up every bit of hope that remained inside me to try to stay encouraged. I wanted my struggle to mean something. I often told myself there was no way I was going through this struggle for nothing. I missed my mom and my sisters like a prisoner misses freedom. I kept a picture of my youngest sister Paige beside my laptop as a reminder of why I had to keep going.

I also asked myself whether I'd made the right decision to move to San Bernardino. When I started making music, Keyden and I said it was for our family. But here I was creating music far away from them. Would my sisters hate me for not being in their lives? Did my mom think I was selfish for moving to San Bernardino?

The only thing that kept my mind from wandering was working. My manager Street Goddess tried to arrange an opportunity for me to get paid by working exclusively with Glasses Malone again. Glasses needed beats for his album, *White Lighting 2*, and she put in her bid for me to produce as much of it as I could. Sensing this was my second opportunity to turn things around, I spent every day producing and sending her two to three beats for Glasses. I did this for almost three months straight. She was convinced that this was the project that was going to change my life forever.

Unfortunately, it never happened. After that third month of making beats and no release date in sight for *WL2*, I felt like I had nothing left to give to music. I knew this was the nature of the business and nobody was at fault, but it still hurt. I wasn't mad at anyone except myself for taking such a risk with my time, and I didn't have any energy to play the industry waiting game anymore.

This was the final straw for me. I was ready to quit music and find a 9-5. Actually, I started to believe that I had truly lost my mind. Just to give you an idea of how crazy and weak I'd become, let me tell you about one lonesome morning that will forever live in my memories.

The morning started off just like any other in the apartment. I ate some leftover burritos from the night before, checked my emails, and started making beats.

Unfortunately, I had made the critical mistake of eating a burrito that'd been left out overnight. Within minutes it was ready to come out the other end. As I got up to use the restroom I noticed we didn't have any toilet paper. In fact, the only paper we had in the apartment was the notebook paper on which we wrote our lyrics and the Del Taco burrito paper. I searched my pockets for money to buy toilet paper from the liquor store across the street. No luck. Nothing in the jeans in my dirty clothes bag and only a dime between the couch cushions.

I finally decided to use the notebook paper.

That's something that'll make you feel like less of a man: wiping your rear end with a rough sheet of college-ruled notebook paper. It made me question how my life had gotten to this point.

> *I questioned my purpose on Earth and my worth to those around me. The more I asked, the more I felt myself losing control.*

My mind wandered for a bit after that last thought. I started repeating over and over in my mind: *How did I get here?!* I questioned my purpose on Earth and my worth to those around me. The more I asked, the more I felt myself losing control.

I jumped on the Internet to try re-establishing control, looking for something to distract myself from my negative thoughts. I stumbled across an article on Facebook that said people were listening to the popular YouTube song, "Friday," by Rebecca Black—then committing suicide for unknown reasons.

I thought, *Maybe I shouldn't be reading this right now.*

But for some reason I continued. The article hinted that the song might have included sadistic, subliminal messaging that inspired suicidal thoughts in its listeners.

Now as absolutely ridiculous as it feels to be writing these words—and as crazy as it probably sounds to you—in the mental state I was in I didn't even question the common sense of that article. The idea that listening to "Friday" could drive someone to commit suicide seemed *real* to me at the time.

What I couldn't see in that moment was that I was quickly losing touch with reality.

The article described the odd behavior that "victims" exhibited before they took their lives, and I saw a little bit of myself in all of them. By the time I reached the end of the article I was completely convinced that I was going to be the next one to kill myself. I had absolutely no control over my thoughts and emotions. It felt that with every passing second the chorus of that song got louder and louder in my head. My heart raced, my palms were sweating, my breathing was short and fast. I started to feel lightheaded.

Then without warning I stood up and quickly opened the front door of the apartment. I took two steps forward and looked over the 2-story balcony to measure the fall. I took about fifteen steps backwards and prepared myself to jump. My heart was beating so fast I was convinced that if I didn't jump a heart attack would kill me anyway.

I braced myself, tears rolling down my eyes, knowing I was completely committed to going through with it. I looked around the room, trying my best not to think about my parents or sisters.

And then something miraculous happened.

The only thing that stopped me from jumping that day was the picture of my baby sister, Paige. In the midst of me freaking out I hadn't realized that the picture had fallen from my computer desk and onto the floor.

I looked around the room again, wiped my eyes, and said out loud, "WHAT THE FUCK ARE YOU DOING, DWAN?"

And I slowly started inching my way back into reality.

All I could think to do at that point was close the door and go to sleep. I didn't want to call or be a burden to anybody. All I wanted to do was sleep.

And that's what I did for the next few hours until Jynxx got home from work.

Until now, I've never told anyone about that day, because it took me years to understand it for myself. My conclusion was that this episode had little or nothing to do with the article or that "Friday" song. What I experienced was a nervous breakdown that could've been triggered by almost anything at that point.

A few days later I showed the article to a friend. He laughed and pointed out that it came from a spoof news website.

I GOT YOUR BACK, CURT

It was a difficult time for all of us in that apartment—Jynxx, Yasin, and myself. But we had each other's backs. We all lacked funds but made up for it in music. Living at that apartment was the first time I was told to simply do what I do best—and somehow make it make me money. On the good days in that apartment, when I sold a few more beats than usual, we ate like fast food kings.

No, things weren't perfect but those circumstances made us stronger and turned us into lifelong brothers. If one of us had money, all of us had money. If one of us had food, all of us had food. That's just the way we ran it.

One night after work, Jynxx wanted to walk to the liquor store. I decided to roll with him. Earlier that day Street Goddess had told me to be on the lookout for the new *Source* magazine because it mentioned my name as a producer on the new Glasses Malone and Mack 10 album.

When we arrived at the liquor store I darted straight for the magazine rack to see if I could find the article. I skimmed straight through the first sixty pages to the album-review section.

And there was my name in the legendary *Source* magazine, under the production credits for a song entitled "Until the Feds Came."

I couldn't believe it—and apparently neither could the liquor store cashier. Here I was dressed in my bummy weekday nightwear, without a haircut, trying to convince the cashier that my name was in his magazine. It also didn't help that I was snapping photos of the article with my cellphone because I couldn't afford the $5 it cost to buy it.

As I struggled to get the perfect angle to snap a picture of the article, Jynxx laughed and offered to buy the magazine for me. A few days later he surprised me by using his company van to stop by Best Buy to buy me a hard copy of the album. I was extremely grateful, even though I found it quite embarrassing. I mean, imagine getting your first major-label placement but being too broke to buy it out of the store!

NEW BEGINNINGS, NECESSARY ENDINGS

My lowest point taught me a lot about myself and what truly mattered to me: my family. I felt like I was out of the loop of their lives so I made it a habit to keep in better touch with them. Beyond that I also felt out of the loop with some of my music-based relationships in Los Angeles.

Without getting into too much detail, there was a dispute between Street Goddess and her former team at TDE. Some of the issues involved in it started to spill over into Twitter and put me right in the middle. This in turn put my relationship with Ab-Soul in jeopardy. In fact, I think the behind-the-scenes turmoil between my manager and TDE is why I wasn't invited to produce any records for Ab's album *Longterm Mentality*. It was the only album in Ab's catalog that I didn't produce a record for, and it bummed me out.

For this and a few other reasons, Street Goddess and I decided to cut our business ties. To this day I absolutely appreciate her and the work and time that she put in on my behalf. I just believe that life was pulling us in opposite directions.

About a year or so later I got the opportunity to repair my relationship with Ab-Soul. When we linked back up it was like we'd never broken off.

"A REBELLION"

I don't regret any of my past setbacks. Motivational speaker Les Brown calls those hard periods in our lives "character building" times. All the things that I endured over those years made me a better artist, a better producer, and a better man. It's my belief that when you listen to music that you interpret as genuinely beautiful, soulful, or even depressing, at the source of that music is a heart that has already endured that emotional state.

> All the things that I endured over those years made me a better artist, a better producer, and a better man.

Think of how a kettle has to get hot before the water in it boils over. I think artistic expression works the same way. *Life* builds up inside you until it boils over. Speaking as a producer, I feel that every time we choose an instrument when creating our music we're making an emotional decision. Each drum tone or piano chord progression is an expression of the emotions embedded deep in our souls—getting so hot that they boil out of us in the form of music.

I had this epiphany as I sat in front of my keyboard hours after my grandfather's funeral in 2011. He was my last surviving grandfather, and he had a heart of gold. He always went out of his way to check up on me and say that if I needed his help he was a phone call away. My pride wouldn't allow me to ask him for that help, but his offer warmed my heart.

I took the news of his passing very hard. I had learned so much from him: my work ethic, for example, the value of a consistent morning ritual, and that a man should never be ashamed to clean the counter or do the dishes for his wife. I also learned how to be an efficient *Price Is Right* contestant.

The evening after his funeral, Noa and Lesa came over to the apartment to chill. Not a lot was said, but I surely appreciated their presence in the room. The last thing I needed was to be alone with my thoughts. I had so many emotions bottled up inside me that I just felt like I needed to make music. As I hooked up my computer and started to work, all the pain, all the sadness, and all the regret flowed through every sound I chose.

> **As I started to work, all the pain, all the sadness, and all the regret flowed through every sound I chose.**

About forty-five minutes later I had an instrumental that would go on to become my next placement with Ab-Soul for a song called "A Rebellion." The song featured the late Alori Joh and was by far one of the most emotional songs on Ab's *Control System* album.

I don't believe that was an accident. Real music is supposed to evoke real emotions. Music is simply the soul boiling over into sound. When you produce with this in mind, there is no way you'll ever miss the mark.

HOW I FEEL ABOUT PLACEMENTS TODAY

Growing up I used to look at placements the way Rick Grimes on the TV show *Walking Dead* looks at abandoned houses: a chance for survival in an industry full of zombies.

I know that every placement I've ever received was a blessing—whether I was paid for it or not. Every single one of those experiences contributed to where I am today. My brother Ab-Soul gave me the opportunity to produce "Tree of Life"—the lead single from his *These*

Days album. My mentor and big brother Murs gave me the opportunity to produce an entire mixtape for him and a song featuring E-40. They both know that I'm always a phone call or an email of beats away when they need me.

> **Music is simply the soul boiling over into sound. When you produce with this in mind, there is no way you'll ever miss the mark.**

But today, when it comes to pursuing placements with other rappers, I don't even bother.

Young producers, here's my take today on placements: know what you truly want before you pursue them. It is my belief that you can have all the money and fame your major-placement heart desires, but one has to come before the other one. It's like the popular chicken or the egg scenario, except the choices are money and notoriety. If you want to get your name out there and circulating through the music industry, by all means do everything in your power to capture that often-elusive placement. However, if you desire to make money first, understand that you may have to take a few alternative routes to placements to accomplish that goal.

After I parted ways with my manager I had a brief stint with a producer collective curated by Ace Pun called The League of Starz. At the time, LOS was a group of six producers who were getting major placements with everyone from Lil Wayne to Chris Brown. Unfortunately, after a year or so it became obvious that I didn't quite fit their sound. I was a sample-based producer in an industry that was rapidly shifting from sampled music to original music without samples.

I came to learn—again—that God had an entirely different path laid out for my career.

<u>Lessons to Take Away from Chapter 11</u>

1. Problems are inevitable. Seek not to get rid of your problems, but seek for better-quality problems. (Which would you rather decide: how to get your music placed or what to use for toilet paper when you don't have any at hand?)

2. Don't let a fear of looking stupid make you afraid to take risks. Failure (and looking stupid) is a necessary step on the path to success.

3. Working hard is important, but your mental and physical health should always remain your number one priority. If you think you might need some help, get it—and don't be embarrassed to ask for it. ALL OF US need help at times.

4. Control your thoughts and you will ultimately control your destiny. If you see the glass as half full instead of half empty, life will present sufficient evidence to support your viewpoint.

5. Placements take time and can be a waiting game; once you've submitted something or put yourself out there, stay busy and focused on the *next* opportunity.

Lessons to Take Away from Chapter 11 (continued)

6. Stay open to opportunities for placements. These opportunities can come from anywhere and anyone. Think back to my friends Robbin and Komboa.

7. Always be ready to deliver your music on demand, no matter your circumstances or shortcomings.

8. Be smart with your money—don't spend what you don't have.

9. Know your worth, or one day someone will determine it for you.

10. Your career is important—but so are the loved ones in your life. Find a happy balance that allows you to spend time with both.

11. Sign up TODAY for your ASCAP or BMI Performing Rights Organization!

CHAPTER 12

SHARE
THE BEAT

"Your beats are your real estate property."

~ *Curtiss King Beats (Me!)*

Over the course of my career, almost every producer I've considered a mentor has had nothing but bad things to say about the business of leasing beats. I listened to them without question because they felt so strongly about the subject.

One argued that selling beats for dirt cheap compromises the integrity of a producer's work. Another said that if just anybody could purchase my beats it would damage the overall value of my brand. Another believed that leasing producers never make it in the music business and that pursuing placements is the only way to go.

I listened to all of them—and was still broke. Was it time for me to go against the grain yet again?

LEASING BEATS

For music producers unfamiliar with the beat-leasing business, allow me to break it down for you.

There exists a world—primarily online and away from the traditional music industry—where producers upload catalogs of their beats and make them available for purchase by the general public. Prices are significantly lower than what an artist will pay or a producer will receive for a typical placement. This is because the clientele are generally unsigned or independent rappers on limited

> *The irony is that I was terrified of compromising my brand's perceived worth but not taking the proper steps behind the scenes to actually make it worth something.*

budgets. Because these customers aren't working with major-label budgets, leasing or test-driving a beat for a significantly lower price is an extremely convenient and cost-efficient option.

Most producers offer three leasing options that allow customers to choose things like their desired beat format (MP3, WAV, Trackouts) and their desired licensing agreement.

In this business, multiple rappers have access to the same beats. If a rapper wants to take a beat off the market he has the option of purchasing the exclusive rights to the beat for a significantly higher price. It's a win-win situation for both sides: artists have access to high-quality production for a lower price and producers earn steady income from their beats.

In retrospect, I wish someone would've explained this business model to me the way that I just explained it to you.

Why did it take me so long to start leasing my beats? I was simply too scared. I was too self-conscious about what my peers would say if

I started leasing my beats after working with respected names like Kendrick Lamar and Ab-Soul. The irony of the situation is that I was terrified of compromising my brand's perceived worth *but not taking the proper steps behind the scenes to actually make it* worth *something.*

Quite frankly, it took me years to understand the psychology of the beat-leasing business.

Now, it's true that over the years I *have* seen producers who lived out some of my mentor's worst-case scenarios. These producers would sell their beats for $10 each and run outrageous bulk deals like "buy 1 get 20 beats free."

But that's hardly a complete picture of the beat-leasing business.

EPIK

One of the first producers I saw speak on the benefits of leasing beats was Epik.

In 2010 I attended the annual, music-related Western Awareness Conference in Los Angeles. I went desperately looking for answers that could help me out of my financial woes. The conference hosted a number of panels with accomplished artists, songwriters, radio personalities, DJs, and producers.

All of my focus was on the producer panel. Epik was on it, and although I didn't know him personally, I'd been told by some mutual friends that he was making a great living doing nothing but selling his beats. I assumed he was selling beats so consistently because he must have first gotten some major placements.

I was wrong. Epik explained to the conference attendees how he made a living selling his beats online to artists all over the world. He discussed how a $100 investment in Soundclick during a time of serious financial struggle helped him launch his own leasing business.

Epik broke down every single step he took and shared how his plan changed his life.

I don't remember anyone else on the panel that day because they all seemed to say the same thing: placements are the way to go. But Epik spoke from a fresh perspective. He gave me hope that there existed a community of producers who didn't need placements to be prosperous.

However, I didn't do much with the information when I left the conference. This was around the time we were being evicted from our townhome in the IE, and back then $100 seemed like a lot to invest into something that I wasn't certain would work.

MY FIRST ACCIDENTAL LEASES

I wouldn't think about leasing beats again until years later, when something crazy happened in San Francisco.

In 2013, legendary underground rapper and Paid Dues founder Murs invited Noa James and me to go on tour with him on behalf of Black Cloud Music. In total, seven of us ended up traveling through twenty-five states and almost fifty-two cities in a two-month span. This was the longest that my girlfriend at the time and I had been away from each other since we'd gotten together. After nearly two months on the road we decided to meet up in San Francisco on one of the last legs of the tour. She carpooled to the Bay Area with a few of my labelmates' girlfriends.

In anticipation, I made plans to get us our own hotel room in San Francisco. While searching for affordable hotels I found a room for the perfect price in the heart of downtown San Francisco. Another labelmate of mine named David May also reserved a room at the same hotel. Our other labelmates were staying closer to the venue of our next show, but they dropped us off first.

The minute we started dragging our luggage down the street towards the entrance of the hotel, a homeless lady popped out in front of us from behind a parked car and stared us down. We stared back, expecting her to ask us for change, but instead she pulled her pants down and started urinating on the sidewalk in front of us. David and I looked at each other in disgust and went into the hotel. As I waited for the desk clerk to check us in, I looked around the lobby and noticed some peculiar things.

For starters, the building looked prehistoric. Paint that was once white was now chipped and dingy yellow. The furniture was run down and ancient. I hoped that the rooms looked much better than the lobby.

When the clerk finally finished processing our information she handed us two silver door keys. No, not two electronic keys that you slide into the hotel door to open it, but two "go-get-the-mop" style janitorial room keys.

We walked down the long hallway toward our rooms; there was a bathroom and kitchen at the end of it. Thinking nothing of this I found my assigned door, inserted the key and opened it up. The first thing I saw were four blank walls, one window with bars on it, no television, no bathroom, and one bed with a roll of toilet paper at the head of it. Apparently, I hadn't booked a room at a hotel—this was a hostel.

David and I looked at each other in dismay. There was no way we could have our girlfriends stay at this place. We marched right back to the front desk to demand a refund. The clerk didn't say a word; she just pointed at a sign that read "NO REFUNDS!"

This was terrible. David and I were both strapped for cash.

I immediately broke out my phone and started searching for other hotels in the area, hoping we could catch a break on a couple of super cheap rooms within walking distance. Unfortunately, there was only one hotel in the area and for some reason it didn't list its prices. We returned our keys to the clerk and dragged our luggage to the next hotel, hoping to secure a room before our girlfriends arrived.

The Courtyard Marriott was a few blocks away. The only rooms they had available were $220 a night. Seeing the dejected look on both of our faces, the front desk clerk leaned in and whispered to us that we could find much better deals online. I whispered back sincerely, "Thank you."

Online I stumbled upon a deal that cut the room down to $135. Now, although this was an amazing price, I only had a total of $50 in my Paypal account.

While we were searching for more discounts our girlfriends arrived at the hotel (we'd phoned to let them know where to find us). It was the first time I'd seen my girl in over two months. As much as I wanted to catch up with her she could tell I was frantic and preoccupied. I updated her on the situation and she offered to help pay for the room, but I kindly declined. It was important to me that I take care of her on this trip.

My mind was moving at a million thoughts per second. *What am I going to do to make this work? How can I flip this situation into a positive?*

Unfortunately my brain wasn't responding. It wasn't until I overheard a lady in the lobby say, "Well, thank God it's Friday right?!" that I got an idea.

Now, by that time, I was selling more beats to my *Dish List*, partly because my sales skills were increasing, and partly, I think, because my beats were getting more diverse due to me traveling across the U.S. So the thought occurred:

What would happen if I sent out an email blast to my Dish List advertising a random Black Friday sale going down today?

Without giving too much thought to the specifics I composed an email that I was hoping could take me from $50 to $135 within the next hour. The email read:

Thank you for supporting Curtiss King Beats. We have a random BLACK FRIDAY sale today on beats for the next hour. $25 for exclusive rights to any of these new beats.

Within ten minutes I started receiving text messages and responses inquiring about my deal. The artists in my list couldn't believe I was offering exclusive rates for so cheap. At that time, I was charging $100 and up for exclusive rights, so this Black Friday deal was a steal.

In less than an hour I cleared over $300 dollars, enough not only for the room but also to get us all pizza.

David ended up calling home for a favor and bought the same room deal.

For some reason that $25 price point made me think about the leasing business again. Three hundred dollars was more money than I made some entire months trying to sell my beats. Yet here I'd just made it in less time than it takes to deliver a pizza. That night I thought: *Is this what the leasing business is like?*

I didn't give it much more thought on that trip because I was too excited that I'd made things work out for us. For some reason, even then, it still didn't click within me that the beat-leasing business was worth looking into.

> *That $25 price point made me think about the leasing business again. In less than an hour I'd made more than I'd done in some entire months.*

BACK TO THE BOTTOM AGAIN?

I returned home a new man after touring with Murs and Black

Cloud Music. I had a new sense of urgency. I'd shown myself I could tough it out on the road. Things were starting to look up for me and my career.

But just as quickly they started to come crashing right back down when the reality of "life-after-tour" set in.

My labelmates and I had been on tour for over two months—without pay. We survived that tour by selling our merchandise. Everything from food to gas to rooms was funded by whatever we sold at our show the night before, and along the way we maxed out our credit cards. So actually we didn't return home just broke, but in debt.

Even worse, my relationship with Jynxx took a turn for the worse while we were on tour together.

Jynxx and I knew each other way too well. On tour we bickered every other week about something petty. Eventually petty arguments became bigger and more personal—so much so that it started to affect the way we conducted business with one another. Within a few months of being back home, I decided to leave the Black Cloud Music label. I didn't have a plan for what to do next but I knew I couldn't wait any longer. My responsibilities were bigger, and life desperately needed me to become more independent.

When I returned home the first few months were rough. My beat sales were slow again. I'd just left my label, and I was up to my neck in debt. I was also staying with my girlfriend and some of her friends. These friends had already done a lot for us by opening their home to us—and really it was my responsibility to take care of my needs.

After having a heart-to-heart with the homeowner, we settled on a reasonable one-month timeline for us to move out. I went into a bit of a frenzy trying to figure out what we were going to do next. I was job hunting relentlessly for something with a consistent paycheck. The only problem was that there was a five-year gap of unemployment on my résumé due to my music career.

Every day brought us closer to when we had to leave. My lady and I were arguing more than ever because we feared the possibility of becoming homeless.

Then I recalled the last time I was this desperate, the time I'd made $300 in less than an hour selling my beats for $25. And I thought, *I need to put my pride aside and start leasing my beats.*

OSYM BEATS

In between filling out job and apartment applications I searched far and wide on the Internet for information about leasing beats. What I found was an overwhelming amount of bullshit. I just didn't know whom or what to believe. Then one night when I was wasting time on Facebook I saw an update from a friend that said, "It's such a blessing to be #1 on SoundClick again!"

> *I remembered the last time I was this desperate, the time I'd made $300 selling my beats in less than an hour. I thought: I need to start leasing my beats.*

That friend was a producer named OSYM Beats. His name is an acronym for Old Soul in a Young Man. I was introduced to his music years before when I used to blog for fun at a website called How2BeFamous. He was always a cool guy when we crossed paths at shows, and we were both from Carson. We didn't chop it up frequently but when we did talk he picked my brain about the music business. He was always smart, sharp, and persistent about accomplishing his goals. Additionally, in 2012 he blessed me with a few beats for my album *Atychiphobia*.

Years had passed since he'd been that young artist looking to soak up game from me. He'd found success for himself in the beat-leasing business after graduating college. I didn't know exactly how successful he was, but judging by his Facebook updates it appeared he was doing well—and a lot better than I was.

But as desperate as I was to make something happen before that month was up, I *still* hesitated to ask OSYM for help. It wasn't until I received a text message from my girl informing me that the car wouldn't start that I decided to put my pride aside. I offered to buy OSYM lunch for the opportunity to pick his brain on the topic of leasing beats. I expected him to do what most producers in Hip Hop would do in that scenario: refuse to share valuable information and hang up. To my surprise, he agreed to meet.

When we met the next day it was too late to go grab lunch, so we connected where I was staying. I explained to OSYM how dire my situation was, how we only had a few weeks before we had to find another place to stay, and how I wanted to learn more about leasing my beats. He just sat there patiently and listened.

When I was done he calmly reassured me that things were going to be alright and that I was just in a temporary storm. He actually said he was glad I'd reached out to him when I did. And best of all he was willing to share his knowledge of the leasing business—the same knowledge that had allowed him to quit his job and create music full time.

He warned me that the information might be a bit overwhelming at first, and that things would have to move fast for me to reach my goal. But he was down to teach me.

Step-by-step I began to build my leasing business: Curtiss King Beats. First came the VIP Soundclick account for $9.99/month. Next the $19.99/month unlimited MyFlashStore (Airbit) account where I uploaded my catalog of beats and gave my customers an instant buying experience.[11]

---

[11] See "What Do I Need to Get Started in the Beat-Leasing Business?" in the Appendix of this book for more information.

Then, since I was already familiar with Photoshop, OSYM offered me a customizable template for my Soundclick website, which I edited the same night. This was a crucial step because it was the first thing potential customers would see upon visiting my page.

Finally OSYM had me compile a folder full of at least fifty beats to sell. He spent a few days with my list and narrowed it down to a solid thirty that he thought would do well. When I asked him his method of determining potential great sellers, he told me it was something that he couldn't explain in words; he just felt it. He assured me that I too would eventually develop this instinct.

After all the preliminary steps were taken care of, OSYM invested $500 into Curtiss King Beats. Besides John, that was more money than anybody had ever invested in my music career, and it made me extremely nervous. Where I'm from, people don't just invest $500 dollars into you without you giving them an arm, leg, and your first-born baby. But he did it without hesitation and negotiated a

> **Step by step I began to build my leasing business: Curtiss King Beats.**

reasonable deal with me that would allow me to pay him back in small increments—25% of my beat sales until I paid him back in full.

The entire process put me in a much calmer place, although I still worked with urgency because time was ticking away. We had to move soon and we still hadn't found a new place. But OSYM's confidence in me helped me find the confidence in myself.

In those final weeks, I started to read a book by Robert Kiyosaki called *Rich Dad, Poor Dad*. That book was crucial in the rewiring of my brain as I began my new journey. It helped me see that for years I was a slave to money. I let money run my life. I let money rule over my happiness. I let it influence so many decisions that it had no business influencing. Reading Robert's story and seeing how much I could relate to it also put me at ease, because he'd gone on to become a multimillionaire.

Unfortunately, my lady didn't understand all this *calm* business I was talking about. She was rightfully worried about our situation, mostly because of her son's well-being. She didn't understand how I could invest the type of money I'd invested into something that didn't promise a return. The more I asked her to trust me, the more frustrated she became—and the more we argued. I understood where she was coming from, but I felt like this was my last hope.

Just a week into the leasing business, I started to see some action. Not enough to get excited about because I had mountains of debt, but it was moving. OSYM and I talked about my progress every day. As I awaited more sales, I continued making new beats. In fact I made more beats in those final weeks than I'd ever done before in our bedroom. From my lady's perspective, I looked selfish and irresponsible. The day was quickly approaching when we had to move out, and here I was making music on my laptop. I tried sharing with her the progress the business was making, but she was too angry with me for not job hunting to listen.

In that first month of the leasing business OSYM led me from making $80-$150 a month to making over $2,000. The month had been so chaotic that I hadn't even noticed how well I was doing. In a way it was frustrating: I'd finally found a way to start generating income, but the only thing I couldn't buy us was more time.

Finally, when all hope seemed lost another friend of ours named Erica opened her apartment doors to us in San Bernardino. We didn't waste any time moving in.

MONEY, MONEY, DUMMY

Life as I knew it would never be the same.

Three months into the business of leasing beats I made over

$12,000. This was the most money I'd ever made in my life. In fact, I made more money in my first four months of leasing beats than I'd made in a total of ten years pursuing placements.

OSYM had been right. Everything turned out just fine. At our new place we only had to pay $200 for rent and our expenses were super low. The beat-leasing business did have a high overhead to maintain, but the return was amazing. For the first time in my life I was making more money than I needed to cover my expenses.

> **I made more money in my first four months of leasing beats than I'd made in ten years pursuing placements.**

Fifty miles away my mom's life was stabilizing as well. She and my sisters moved into their own apartment in Long Beach. Things seemed to finally be falling back into place for us both. Most importantly, I was finally making enough money to send some my mom's way without worrying if I could also take care of myself.

And while we're on the subject, I was spending a lot of money on myself.

Apparently I'd missed that important detail in the *Rich Dad, Poor Dad* book where he clearly states the importance of not purchasing a bunch of liabilities. During that time, I was spending money uncontrollably on new shoes, clothes, cellphones, and music equipment. I felt like I was making up for lost time.

I tried my best to convince myself that my financial literacy was improving every time I made more money. But the truth of the matter is that I was financially illiterate. OSYM tried to warn me to save for a rainy day, but my current wins were blinding me. I was spending my money just as fast as it came in.

Why? I think because I was spending my money *emotionally*. At this point, money represented a form of freedom for me. No longer would I be unable to afford the combo with my fast food meals. No longer would I have to put a few dollars in my gas tank just to barely make it back and forth between destinations. No longer would I have to go through the embarrassing process of bringing a bucket of change to the supermarket and loudly pour it into the Coinstar machine.

This was my new life, and I was doing my best to spend as much money as it took to erase my bad memories.

I think I knew I had a spending problem when I went to Target to get a high. Next door to my apartment was a Target where I spent a lot of time. Having money felt so good that I would simply walk from aisle to aisle reminding myself that I could afford to buy anything I desired. Ninety percent of the time I wouldn't even buy anything. Just knowing I could afford it gave me a high.

As you've probably guessed by now, all that spending caught up with me. And although I had more cash, it didn't necessarily mean I had better credit. I wasn't paying off any of my old debts and I was spending money faster than I saved it, so having money actually put me into a deeper financial hole. I also had new liabilities connected to my business overhead. For

> **For the next few months, the kid who hated math growing up did inventory analysis spreadsheets.**

example, advertisements for my online business were at least 40-45 percent of my income, so technically I wasn't earning as much as I thought I was. Plain and simple I was spending money like an idiot.

LIVE BELOW YOUR MEANS

Again I turned to OSYM for advice. I asked him how to become more financially responsible in the beat-leasing business, and he offered some powerful insights. One thing he told me many times was that it was up to me to live below my means. I also picked the brain of

Art Barz, one of my former Black Cloud Music labelmates. Art was one of the most financially literate friends I had. He echoed OSYM's exact sentiments: save money from every beat sold and live below your means. Both of them also gave me suggestions for a handful of books to dig into to help me turn my bad habits around.

For the next few months, the kid who hated math growing up did inventory analysis spreadsheets. The guy who was once terrible about his credit now had a secured credit card which promised to help build his credit score. I started saving a percentage of every one of my sales and depositing it into my bank account.

OSYM's and Art's advice had come at the perfect time. Because of some unforeseen circumstances, we all had to move out of that apartment in San Bernardino within a month.

This time around I was a lot less stressed out. Money was no longer my biggest issue. Unfortunately, my poor credit score *did* mean a lot to potential landlords. My girl and I searched tirelessly for apartment managers willing to work with our situation. And by the grace of God we found something perfect for us.

One of my girl's family members worked at a rental company that helped out families with bad credit. Through them we got a listing of rental properties in the IE, one of which was a one-story, three-bedroom house with a huge backyard, and a one-car garage. The only challenge was that the rent was $1345. This was steep, but we agreed to give it a chance.

For the next few weeks I worked like a machine to gather up the $2600 we needed to secure the home. In the first week, I saved $900 from my sales. The second week, I pocketed about $400. The third week, God threw me a massive alley-oop.

A customer from Minnesota sent me an email inquiring about seven beats he wanted to purchase exclusively. At the time my exclusive prices were $350 a beat, but I offered discounts for any customer who purchased in bulk. I needed this order to happen. I told myself that if I could at least get him to agree to $2000 we were going to be alright. We ended up landing on $2300.

We finally had enough money to secure the home.

A week later we moved in. After years of sharing very small spaces, we finally had rooms to call our own. The icing on the cake? There was a third room I could convert into my home studio/office space.

Life wasn't always perfect in that house, but it was far more stable than it had been in previous years. Although that relationship eventually came to an end, there were still some very valuable lessons

> *If you've been blessed with a dream or a vivid image of the goals you NEED to accomplish, you have simultaneously been burdened with the responsibility to see them through to the end.*

that I learned during this period. There wasn't a day I woke up and didn't thank the man upstairs. Even though we were renting, the experience taught me a very valuable lesson about the power of gratitude. Moving into that home brought my chaotic life a lot of overdue peace.

Producers, this is a lifestyle and career that requires a lot of your energy, time, patience, and faith. More importantly, it sometimes requires just as much energy from the people around you—whether they signed up for it or not. If producing is your dream, this is important for you to remember.

THE PROSPEROUS PRODUCER

You and I have been given this gift called life, and we don't know when we'll have to return it. If you've been blessed with a dream or a vivid image of the goals you NEED to accomplish, you have simultaneously been burdened with the responsibility to see them through to the end.

Fast forward to the present day and you'll see that I have chosen to experience my prosperity in a much humbler way. It's just me and the new love of my life, Domunique, in a one-bedroom apartment, surrounded by endless inspiration, books, trampolines, vegan food, and walls draped with posters of my heroes. It's a smaller space than I'm used to, but it's more than enough room for me to focus on the business at hand: CurtissKingBEATS.com.

I am thankful that it took me as long as it did to get here. I am humbled to be considered a Prosperous Producer by so many of my peers. There were times when I almost lost it all. Hell, there have been times even in the last year that I thought I was going to lose it all, but by the grace of God I kept it together. With the strong support system that is my family and friends, I was able to make it out of some dire circumstances.

The most beautiful part of it all?

I'm just getting started.

Lessons to Take Away from Chapter 12

1. Be wise with your money, even (especially!) when you're making a lot of it.
2. Live below your means.
3. Never be afraid to ask for help.
4. Be open to new ideas and sources of revenue; don't just assume other people's opinions are right for you. (Leasing beats gave me my independence and dignity back.)
5. Never forget the family and friends who support you in your pursuit of your dreams, even when they didn't sign on for it.

CHAPTER 13

THE PRODUCENEUR

MUSIC PRODUCER + ENTREPRENEUR = *PRODUCENEUR*

T he beat-leasing business gave me a fresh start on life, letting me breathe a kind of financial oxygen that hadn't been available to me for most of my life up to that point.

I haven't worked a traditional 9-5 for the last nine years of my life. I've been leasing beats for five years now, and every year it gets better financially than the year before it.

My parents never taught me what to do in the event that I became financially prosperous through music or anything else, but I don't fault them for that. Not many of us are taught how to handle abundance. Most times we're just taught to appreciate it (which is also a good thing to do).

But the beat-leasing business gave me the opportunity to do things differently.

I've learned a lot about how to run a small business. I've read dozens of books written by entrepreneurs and thinkers like Tony Robbins, Les Brown, Gary Vaynerchuk, Grant Cardone, Jim Rohn, John C. Maxwell, Robert Kiyosaki, Seth Godin, Tai Lopez, Don Miguel Ruiz, Dave Ramsey, Darren Hardy and many more. I've listened to countless hours of podcasts by entrepreneurs such as John Lee Dumas of EoFire and Tim Ferris of the Tim Ferris Podcast. I've consumed an obsessive amount of keynote speeches and TED videos over the years.

I've done it all in the hopes of finding an answer to the million-dollar question that for many years I didn't even know I wanted answered:

What is my purpose in life?

I was always taught that the key to life is obtaining unconditional happiness. Confused about exactly what happiness *was*, I went on a wild goose chase trying to find it in achievements and material possessions. Even at the heart of my initial commitment to start making music there existed a goal of material possessions I wanted for my family.

The problem was that I was equating my happiness with *things* and with what those *things* could do for me and the people I love. Instead of spending more time *loving* my loved ones and making the necessary sacrifices that *showed* how much I loved them, I chose to selfishly pursue my dream.

In other words, my dream was my choice. By choosing music as the vehicle to make that dream come true I simultaneously chose to take on all the pros and cons of that path. I could have been anything in this life but I chose to become a rapper and a producer. A mentor of mine named Sallis once told me I have a habit of complicating the simple things in life. He said if I truly wanted to buy my mom the house of her dreams, or to buy a bunch of material possessions, I should have gotten a job that pays better than music.

Now he was being partly sarcastic, but there was a lot of truth in what he was saying. My choice reveals that I thought music was truly worth pursuing. The struggles I endured didn't have to happen. I could've had the financial freedom I have today doing something completely different. But the question is, would it have given my life a sense of purpose?

Would it have made me happy?

V-A-L-U-E

November 27th, 2015, I was walking around Downtown Disney after going to Murs's show at the House of Blues Anaheim. The high of being my own man and having my own money was now just my normal life—but something felt off.

It wasn't that I was ungrateful. It was that I felt like something was missing in my life. Even though I finally had the life I thought I wanted after years of trials and tribulations, for some reason I still wasn't happy.

A few days later I received some bad financial news while in my studio and it hit me harder than usual. I stood up and yelled, "I'M TOO DAMN SMART TO BE THIS FINANCIALLY STUPID! WHEN DO I CATCH A BREAK!?"

With that I felt myself falling deeper and deeper into another slump. This feeling lasted for weeks until I finally decided to check out a book that Art Barz had repeatedly suggested I read: *The Go-Giver* by Bob Burg and John David Mann.

The fictional story follows a businessman named Joe as he gets his introduction to the true meaning of giving and learns what the word "value" really means—and why it's imperative to every human being's success in life. I listened to the audiobook in one sitting and it lit a fire under me that's been burning ever since.

If you don't gain anything else from my book, please listen to what I'm sharing with you right now.

Our purpose in life is to give value to one another.

Now, don't get it twisted. Value isn't just about money. Value is in the eye of the beholder, and we all have something of value to offer one another. Giving value is more than just the right thing to do; it is literally a prerequisite for your success. No matter what success means to you, value is a necessary ingredient.

What does that mean?

It means that if you desire to make two million dollars, you must find a way to provide something of value that two million people are willing to pay at least a dollar for. Entrepreneur Jeff Olson wrote in his book *The Slight Edge* that we as humans are paid based upon the size of the problems that we solve. If we have the responsibility of deciding whether or not the canned

> **Our purpose in life is to give value to one another.**

foods should get bagged above or below the bread, we get paid according to the significance of that problem.

This concept and many more flipped a light switch in my brain. For years, all I thought about was how I was going to take care of my family and get to the money. I repeat: I gave money too much power and control over my decisions. I should have been asking this question: how can I provide more value to my customers?

This line of thinking honestly changed my life.

I remember listening to my favorite podcast—*EoFire* by John Lee Dumas—religiously during this time. Every morning John would interview entrepreneurs and ask them the same crucial questions: What are your streams of revenue? What was your lowest entrepreneurial moment? And so on. The question that always got my attention was about how these entrepreneurs generated their income. The more I listened to their answers the more I started to see a pattern develop. What did at least 95 percent of the entrepreneurs cite as one of their streams of income?

TEACHING

That's right: teaching. Hearing these multimillionaires talk about how important teaching was to their success was shocking to me. I started to connect the dots that *The Go-Giver* had laid out, and this made me think about how difficult it was for me to learn my own way in the early days of my career. I had to ask: even though Hip Hop is a genre that prides itself on independence and rags-to-riches rap stories, why weren't we giving each other more value like other entrepreneurs were doing?

Were we as rappers and producers busier than those multimillionaires? Were we too good to teach each other? Were we too scared that our peers would steal our ideas? How can we criticize kids for being lost if we aren't willing to teach them?

When I answered these questions for myself I felt a bit embarrassed for my culture. I also felt like I should be doing more for the Hip Hop culture I loved so much. I'd been blessed to meet so many influential people and learn so many valuable lessons in my career, so why wasn't I sharing my *own* knowledge?

The answer wasn't that I was worried someone was going to steal my ideas or compete with me. It was because I had so many self-doubts about stepping into the shoes of a "teacher." Who did I think I was? Such audacity!

But then I thought about a quote by John Lee Dumas:

> *An **expert** witness in the court of law is defined as somebody who knows more than other people in the courtroom.*

Given that straightforward standard, I was able to think about all the occasions where I had actually *been* the expert in a "courtroom" full of rappers and producers. Especially when they were younger rappers and producers. This obviously didn't make me better than them. I was just the default expert in certain crowds based on my experiences and story.

All my life I've been a problem solver for myself and others. One thing experience has taught me is that if you're an efficient problem solver, you often KNOW more than most people in the area in which you're solving problems. And I was always taught that the more you KNOW the more you OWE.

I started thinking about the divide between the younger and older generations of Hip Hop. The older producers get mad at the younger

> *We all have value to give to one another, but this will never happen unless we're willing to break bread with the other side.*

producers for sounding the same, while the younger producers get mad at the OGs for never taking the time to show them the way. Myself? At the moment I'm dead smack in the middle of them, trying my best to understand both sides of the argument.

In my gut I know we're fighting over the wrong things. We all have value to give to one another, but this will never happen unless we're willing to break bread with the other side.

So instead of choosing to be part of the problem, I chose to contribute my energy to a solution. I started sharing my information in a way that my industry wasn't used to. I spoke from the heart, passing along every single necessary detail I possessed to help others in my industry win. Maybe because the information came from a source you don't usually get to hear from—a middle-aged rapper/producer—I felt like the only voice both sides were willing to listen to. Sure, there might have been a little bit of risk sharing all my "secrets," but it was more than worth it to help and motivate others.

Little did I know when I started doing it that this was my purpose all along.

I recorded a video on my iPhone called "The Biggest Lie in Hip Hop" in which I spoke for six minutes along the lines of what's in the above few paragraphs. That video reached more than 76,000 viewers on Facebook and YouTube in less than twenty-four hours. That was more viewers than any content with my name on it had ever achieved.[12]

As this book goes to print it marks the two-year anniversary of my life-changing decision to share what I have to offer. Since I made that decision I've enjoyed the most lucrative year of my life. Last year my beats and other music-related endeavors generated over six figures in sales. My Curtiss King TV YouTube channel is generating consistent income off the strength of my Artist Marketing 911, Producer Motivation 911, and #Curtspiration videos. My videos have been viewed over three million times. And although I'm proud of those numbers, they mean nothing to me without my sanity and happiness. My family is happy and that makes me happy.

Scan the QR code to hear "The Biggest Lie in Hip Hop."

MY FATHER AND ME

And speaking of family, I'm sure a few of you are curious how my relationship is with my dad today.

It's the best it's ever been.

I often say that the man I am today is the result of my trials, my triumphs—and who my father inspired me to be. When I first began making music I wanted his acceptance for taking on a dream very different from his own. After a few years of growth, the next thing I

---

[12] "The Biggest Lie Told in Hip Hop."
https://www.youtube.com/watch?v=7UUJQYnteCA

wanted was his support for my dreams. Instead, I interpreted his constant critiques of my career choice as his way of expressing disappointment in me.

But was it disappointment or was it love? And, if he gave my music career the support I wanted him to, would I have been half as driven as I was to accomplish my goals?

I love my dad and the relationship we have today. The older I get the more I see his mannerisms in my own. It took me years of working through my own personal anger and bitterness to realize he just wanted the best for me. His parenting style made it hard for me to see that it was his way of trying to protect me from the painful experiences I'd endured. But at this stage of my journey I can say that those experiences made me a man that my dad can say he is proud of.

MY JOURNEY

I'm happy for every one of those painful experiences.

Along the way my anger led me to pain. My pain led me to bitterness. My bitterness led me to hopelessness. My hopelessness led me to motivation. My motivation led me to inspiration. My inspiration led me to meditation. My meditation led me to gratitude, and that led me to prosperity and happiness.

You don't become a Prosperous Producer just quietly treading along. Be prepared to trip over a few cracks in the pavement along the way.

This year I made the decision to be unconditionally happy, and this has led me to my own fulfillment.

That, in my eyes, is what truly makes me a Prosperous Hip Hop Producer.

APPENDIX: RESOURCES FOR
THE PROSPEROUS
HIP HOP PRODUCER

W hat follows are some Prosperous Producer 101 materials to help get you started.

This is just the tip of the iceberg. There's lots more where this came from at:

YOUTUBE: CURTISSKINGTV

Search: *Producer Motivation 911 and Curtspiration or scan the QR Code below.*

WHAT DO I NEED TO GET STARTED IN THE BEAT-LEASING BUSINESS?

1. **Stack Up Your Beats! (30-50 Beats)**

The Purpose: Stack the MP3, WAV, and Trackout versions of at least 30-50 beats to start your business. Opening a beat store with only a handful of beats is like a grocery store opening with only a cereal aisle—in other words, you don't appear to be open and ready to serve your customers. Stack your bangers up!

2. **Airbit Account at Airbit.com ($19.99 per month)**

The Purpose: Sign up for an Airbit account and upload your beats so that you can create an instant buying experience for your customers. I use my Airbit account not only as an e-commerce tool, but also as a way to back up my catalog online in the event my hard drive crashes.

3. **Soundclick VIP Page at Soundclick.com ($9.99 per month)**

The Purpose: Sign up for a Soundclick account so that you can create a landing page/website and advertise your beats daily to thousands of rappers and singers worldwide. Get the VIP account so that you can customize your landing page and make it look presentable to potential customers.

4. **XLAY Layouts at Xlay.vision ($25-40 one-time fee)**

The Purpose: Purchase a custom Soundclick page layout from XLAY so that your presentation is appealing to buyers when they visit your VIP page. *Hands down some of the greatest customer service I have ever received!*

17 REASONS WHY YOUR BEATS AREN'T SELLING

Reason 1: You Don't Have Your Own Music Producer Website

The first major obstacle that music producers encounter when they choose to sell their beats online is building a website. Most up-and-coming producers make the fatal mistake of settling for selling their beats on third-party beat-selling websites or exclusively through email. Now in the beginning there's nothing wrong with handling your business through these platforms. I myself have relied upon beat stores with existing traffic to help drive sales to my beats. The only problem is that it isn't sustainable. Websites come and go all the time (e.g., Myspace & possibly SoundCloud). Therefore it's not wise to rely on them for your beat-selling business.

Additionally, what message do you think you're sending your potential customers when you don't own your own URL? This can raise questions in their minds like: *You couldn't afford to purchase a $12 URL? Are you not a professional? Are you not reliable?* It's much better to be able to direct them to your own personal website.

Reason 2: Your Website Takes too Long to Load Up

Say perhaps you DO have a website. Let's say your website

actually looks pretty damn good. Does it take an eternity to load up on a customer's first visit? If it does, this could easily be a reason why potential customers aren't purchasing your beats. A study conducted by Kissmetrics found that over **40 percent of customers will abandon your website if it takes longer than three seconds to load.**[13]

First impressions are everything. If a customer excitedly visits your website looking to buy beats, the amount of time it takes to load that beautiful website can very easily discourage them from buying. This isn't to say you need to create a simplistic, tofu-colored landing page with a beat store. You'll still want to take your time creating a visually pleasing website. However, you must know when to sacrifice aesthetics in the name of sales.

Bottom line: cut the unnecessary dead weight on your website. Eliminate the huge HD YouTube videos on your home page. Eliminate the Star Wars-inspired flash effects that crash older PCs when they attempt to load your page. In this case, less is much more.

Reason 3: Your Website Isn't Visually Clear to Your Buyer

How easily can customers read your website? Are the fonts too small? Is the background too distracting from the text? Is the font color bleeding or blending in too much with the background color? Did you choose the correct fonts/colors for your brand and are they conveying the proper message?

Color and font psychology are CRUCIAL!

Wait, color and font have a psychology?

YES! Google "color psychology" and "font psychology" now and at least glance over a few of the charts that come up. It's remarkable

---

[13] "Kissmetrics Blog." How Loading Time Affects Your Bottom Line. Accessed January 07, 2018. https://blog.kissmetrics.com/loading-time/.

how many of our buying decisions are affected by the colors and fonts we see every day. For example, the color combination of red and yellow has been scientifically proven to make you thirsty and hungry. Now take a second and think about how many fast-food restaurants utilize that colorway. Think back to the times you weren't even thinking about being thirsty until you passed a vending machine with the image of a bright-red cola sitting on top of sky-blue ice cubes.

I feel like the popular Hip Hop acronym C.R.E.A.M. should be updated to "COLOR Rules Everything Around Me." Color runs through and influences our decision-making processes. So ask yourself, if you use the colors yellow and black—which usually signify *caution* or *danger*—on your website, are you communicating messages that elicit hesitation in your visitors rather than an eagerness to buy? (Don't get me wrong: yellow and black might be great colors for your personal brand—I'm just saying *be aware* of what effects colors can have and use them accordingly.)

Also, let's not overlook the importance of our fonts. Can you imagine a poster for a light-hearted children's movie done in the font of a hockey-mask killer horror movie? Of course not, and that's why font psychology is just as important when you're attempting to convey your brand message through your website. Even with good intentions in mind, we can subconsciously give our customers the wrong message if we aren't familiar with the emotions we associate with certain colors and fonts.

Reason 4: Your Website Doesn't Have a Mobile Option

Have you created a website that gives customers who prefer to purchase beats from their iPhones, iPads, and Androids an option to buy? Having a mobile option in today's world is non-negotiable. IT IS A MUST! Most third-party beat stores offer mobile stores for producers because over the last few years the demand has been too high to ignore. You can't rely on rappers to remember to check out your beats whenever they return to their laptops. You must offer a mobile option, or *at least* create a website that works well on all mobile devices to maximize your beat-selling efforts.

Reason 5: Your Beat Store Is too Low Down on Your Website

Is the beat store that showcases your beats too LOW on your website? That is, when people check out your site, do they have to scroll down too far to find the beats you have for sale? After all, your customers come first and foremost to hear your beats.

As common sense as this may sound, you'd be surprised at how many producers complicate this step. I've seen producers bombard visitors to their sites with extended biographies, photos and mixing services before presenting them with the very product they came to the website looking for.

GET THE PEOPLE TO YOUR BEAT STORE!

Most customers aren't interested in your latest YouTube "Rapper Type Beat" or your embedded SoundCloud player. Most of your customers are on your website for your **beats**. This obstacle alone can frustrate impatient buyers. You have about a ten- to fifteen-second window to make an impression on a curious buyer. Why not give your beats their best possible chance at being heard and searched through?

Reason 6: Your Instant Beat Store Doesn't Play Automatically

When rappers visit your website, does your beat store play automatically? It should! Having your beats play automatically forces your customers not only to interact with your beat store, but it also gets them familiar with how it works. Having your potential customer interact with the same store that they'll eventually have to purchase from is crucial.

You must take into consideration the fact that not everyone knows how to work your website. Sometimes it's necessary for you to simulate the process for them so that it doesn't become an obstacle in the way of them making a purchase.

Reason 7: You Don't List Your Buying Instructions Step by Step

What if one of your website visitors just so happens to fall in love with one of your beats? Do they know how to purchase it? Have you listed the buying instructions clearly so that they know how to purchase from you? If not, upload images or text that walk your potential customer step by step through the buying process. Even better is a video that shows your visitor how to purchase from you. Human beings are generally classified as either visual or auditory learners, so it's up to you to provide them with the right kind of stimulation for both styles of learning and make your buying process crystal clear.

Reason 8: You Haven't Clearly Listed Your Leasing Terms

If a rapper leases your beat, are they allowed to make a music video with their final product? If a singer leases your beat is there a limitation on how many sales they can make off their final song?

My point is, do your customers know exactly what they're getting when they invest in your beats? Many customers make their buying decisions based upon the terms you offer with each of your beat leases. So it's important for you to clearly list those terms on your website.

Would you pay for a service without knowing what you're getting? Every customer is different, so it's important for you to provide as much relevant information as you can along with their buying experience. Finding your leasing terms shouldn't be an Easter egg hunt for your customers. A link to your terms should be clearly accessible on your homepage.

Reason 9: You Don't Have Enough Beats on Your Website

Have you uploaded enough beats on your website for customers to choose from? How many beats is enough? I typically suggest producers have anywhere from thirty to fifty beats in their beat stores. Having only a handful of beats can give the impression that you're an amateur or not serious about your beat-leasing business. Either of those two impressions will discourage your potential customer from investing in your business.

Would you purchase from a supermarket with only four items? Of course not! So why would you expect to make sales if your store doesn't look like it's ready to sell? My suggestion is that you stack up your beats and then proceed with business. And take your time with this process! Don't rush your product in the name of a numerical goal. Quality always wins in the end.

Reason 10: Your Pricing Is Inconsistent

Although it may be tempting to price your FAVORITE beats at a higher leasing price than the rest of your catalog, don't do it. Congruency and cohesiveness is not only important for the appearance of your website but also for the presentation of your pricing. It should be one of your main goals to instill buying confidence in your potential customer. Having a uniform pricing system is vital for this goal.

Also, you don't want to give your customers the idea that any of your beats are less valuable than others. Doing this will bring out the price-hagglers and penny-pinchers. Every beat holds its own value to your potential customers and *they are the ones buying*. A beautiful beat is in the eye of the beholder.

Reason 11: Your Customer Doesn't Know How to Contact You

When many rappers are buying (especially for the first time), one of their biggest worries is "What if something goes wrong?!" Try for a second to put yourself in their shoes. Have you ever tried to purchase something extremely expensive online only to have something go wrong on the product checkout page? The first thing most of us want to do is confirm that the company received our order. This is especially true when we see that our credit card got charged for it. Your customers expect and deserve the same level of comfort from you. Clearly list your contact information in multiple places on your site to alleviate that paranoia within your customers.

Reason 12: You Don't Have Your Buyers' Visual Confidence

Have you ever wondered why professional websites always seem to include those "100% Money-Back Guarantee" badges? Well, it's much more than just a fancy icon to make their websites look official. These badges are visual tools that give customers the confidence to pull out their credit cards and buy from you. Not having these badges can cause you to miss out on many great opportunities.

Reason 13: You Don't Have an Email List

Every customer has different buying habits. Not every customer visiting your website for the first time is looking to buy beats from you. Some customers will listen to your beats and plot on purchasing from you in the future. Some customers might be just interested enough to join an email list that notifies them of your new beats. Consider that many rappers buy beats from many different leasing websites. Some rappers go on a beat-leasing shopping spree and don't remember every producer they've purchased from. Additionally, there are rappers who may purchase from your website and never visit you again UNLESS they are on your email list.

Services like MailChimp and GetResponse have made it waaaay easy to set up an email list and launch amazing email campaigns. In short, keep your customers and potential customers in the loop of your latest productions and they will repay you—in visits and dollars.

Reason 14: Does Your Website Offer too Many Services?

In today's music industry, many music producers have received the memo that it requires more than just making beats to make a decent living in this business. Many music producers offer engineering services, drum kits, and a myriad of additional helping hands to the customers they serve. However, just because you offer these services doesn't mean you should showcase ALL of them on your website's homepage. Doing so can often confuse customers about what exactly they should pay attention to first. If you are creating a beat-selling website, focus on the beats first and simplify the presentation. Then, perhaps maybe down the page or in a menu option, offer links that direct customers to your other services.

Reason 15: Do You Have a Unique Sound?

As a music producer, do your beats sound unique? Is your uniqueness somehow expressed through your branding (logo, font, color)? If customers must dig deep for what makes you different from other producers, why shouldn't they skip over your website like the last ten they've visited? Focus on your strengths, and on only improving those weaknesses that hinder the growth of your strengths.

Reason 16: Are You Marketing the Right *Types of* Beats?

If you happen to market your beats using the Jay-Z-type beat or Rick Ross-type beat strategy, are you sure that those artists properly represent your sound? Many times, producers have the right intentions when using a famous rapper's image and brand to appeal to customers that match their sound, but they miss the mark when choosing the RIGHT famous rappers to market. Sit with your beats and give yourself a reality check. Ask friends and other music listeners for their opinions on who they hear over your beats. You might be surprised how informed your little sister or brother are about the subject. Marketing the wrong TYPES of beats can attract the wrong customers. That alone can hinder your bottom line.

Reason 17: You Don't Have a Call to Action on Your Website

Lastly, what do you want your customers to do when they visit your website? Follow you on Twitter? Subscribe to your YouTube channel? Sign up to your email list? It is very important for you to make that objective as clear as possible to your potential customer. I personally suggest embedding a social media button, such as the Facebook "LIKE" thumb or the Twitter "FOLLOW ME" feature near the top of your page. The purpose here is to give your customers something to do or commit to even if they choose not to invest in your beats that day.

There's lots more available at:

CurtissKingBeats.com

Check it out for online classes, beats, drum kits, merchandise and more.

ABOUT THE AUTHOR

D 'wan "Curtiss King" Howard is an award-winning Hip Hop producer, rapper and entrepreneur whose work has captured the hearts and ears of listeners and creators around the world. He's produced music for elite Hip Hop artists like Kendrick Lamar, Ab-Soul, E-40, and Murs, and for corporate giants MTV, VH1, and VANS Apparel. He is an American Advertising Award recipient for his production on the popular online video game *APB: Reloaded.*

Curtiss is the founder of the six-figure beat-leasing business Curtiss King Beats. He offers original music production, sound kits, and online courses at curtisskingbeats.com. His weekly YouTube videos have generated over 3 million views, fueled by a following of dedicated rappers and producers eager to learn from his experience in the music industry.

Curtiss' own music catalog includes twelve albums as a rapper and producer, two of which charted in the top five Hip Hop albums in the country.

Find out more at curtisskingbeats.com.

Publisher's Catalogue

The Prosperous Series

#1 The Prosperous Coach: Increase Income and Impact for You and Your Clients (Steve Chandler and Rich Litvin)

#2 The Prosperous Hip Hop Producer: My Beat-Making Journey from My Grandma's Patio to a Six-Figure Business (Curtiss King)

* * *

Devon Bandison

Fatherhood Is Leadership: Your Playbook for Success, Self-Leadership, and a Richer Life

Sir Fairfax L. Cartwright

The Mystic Rose from the Garden of the King

Steve Chandler

37 Ways to BOOST Your Coaching Practice: PLUS: the 17 Lies That Hold Coaches Back and the Truth That Sets Them Free

50 Ways to Create Great Relationships

Business Coaching (Steve Chandler and Sam Beckford)

Crazy Good: A Book of CHOICES

Death Wish: The Path through Addiction to a Glorious Life

Fearless: Creating the Courage to Change the Things You Can

RIGHT NOW: Mastering the Beauty of the Present Moment

The Prosperous Coach: Increase Income and Impact for You and Your Clients (The Prosperous Series #1) (Steve Chandler and Rich Litvin)

Time Warrior: How to defeat procrastination, people-pleasing, self-doubt, over-commitment, broken promises and chaos

Wealth Warrior: The Personal Prosperity Revolution

Kazimierz Dąbrowski

Positive Disintegration

The Philosophy of Essence: A Developmental Philosophy Based on the Theory of Positive Disintegration

Charles Dickens

A Christmas Carol: A Special Full-Color, Fully-Illustrated Edition

James F. Gesualdi

Excellence Beyond Compliance: Enhancing Animal Welfare Through the Constructive Use of the Animal Welfare Act

Janice Goldman

Let's Talk About Money: The Girlfriends' Guide to Protecting Her ASSets

Christy Harden

Guided by Your Own Stars: Connect with the Inner Voice and Discover Your Dreams

I Heart Raw: Reconnection and Rejuvenation Through the Transformative Power of Raw Foods

Curtiss King

The Prosperous Hip Hop Producer: My Beat-Making Journey from My Grandma's Patio to a Six-Figure Business (The Prosperous Series #2)

David Lindsay

A Blade for Sale: The Adventures of Monsieur de Mailly

Abraham H. Maslow

The Psychology of Science: A Reconnaissance .

Being Abraham Maslow (DVD)

Maslow and Self-Actualization (DVD)

Albert Schweitzer

Reverence for Life: The Words of Albert Schweitzer

William Tillier

Personality Development Through Positive Disintegration: The Work of Kazimierz Dąbrowski

Margery Williams

The Velveteen Rabbit: or How Toys Become Real

Colin Wilson

New Pathways in Psychology: Maslow and the Post-Freudian Revolution

Join our Mailing List:
www.MauriceBassett.com

MAURICE BASSETT

Printed in Great Britain
by Amazon